Hooked by the BBC 4-in-1 Bundle

A Cuckolding Fantasy, Exploring Boundaries,
Shady Business,
Naughty Desires

Amber Carden

CHAPTER ONE: Sleepless Nights 1
CHAPTER TWO: Endless Worries 7
CHAPTER THREE: Unveiling Fantasies 14
CHAPTER FOUR: Surrounding Control 21
CHAPTER FIVE: Coital Bliss 26
CHAPTER SIX: A New Identity 31
CHAPTER SEVEN: Mingling Desires 37
CHAPTER EIGHT: The Conversation 46
CHAPTER NINE: The Invitation 53
CHAPTER TEN: The Next Step 61
CHAPTER ELEVEN: Dangerous Dealings 69
CHAPTER TWELVE: The Confrontation 77
CHAPTER THIRTEEN: The Proposal 84
CHAPTER FOURTEEN: The Unveiling 91
CHAPTER FIFTEEN: A Dangerous Proposition 97
CHAPTER SIXTEEN: Uninvited Guests 104
CHAPTER SEVENTEEN: The Indecent Proposal 111
CHAPTER EIGHTEEN: A Dangerous Choice 117
CHAPTER NINETEEN: Bound and Blindfolded 123
CHAPTER TWENTY: Unfinished Business 129
CHAPTER TWENTY-ONE: Reawakened Desires 134
CHAPTER TWENTY-TWO: Strange Loyalty 141
CHAPTER TWENTY-THREE: Revelations 147
CHAPTER TWENTY-FOUR: Rekindling the Thrill 154
CHAPTER TWENTY-FIVE: Rekindling the Thrill 161
CHAPTER TWENTY-SIX: The Orgy 168

CHAPTER ONE: Sleepless Nights

Mike lay awake in his bed with his wife of fifteen years beside him. He could hear the sound of her breathing and wondered how she could sleep so soundly when he was finding it difficult to close his eyes.

He had come in late again from work like he had done so many times in the past. Before, his wife would stay awake and confront him whenever he came back, shouting at him for leaving her alone for hours. But today, she hadn't. He came back to find her sleeping in bed, not even flinching when he slid into bed with her.

He wondered what that meant, was she tired of him? Was she cheating? He couldn't know. He looked at the time, it was 2:45 am. She was sleeping so soundly, maybe it was because she had slipped out and gotten fucked to completion before he came in. He shook those thoughts out of his mind, it had been fifteen years and she hadn't cheated before, why would she start now?

He turned over to face his wife, taking in her blonde hair and curvy frame, and leaned over, sniffing her hair slightly. He didn't smell anyone else on her but what he did smell was that lavender perfume he loved so much. He felt his dick throb and he got the intense desire to lean over and kiss her neck.

He did just that, giving her soft kisses on the neck to wake her up. She roused slightly but stayed asleep, making Mike feel a little frustrated. He could feel his dick getting harder and he wanted his wife, he wanted her now.

He came closer to her and kissed her neck then sucked on it, hard enough to leave a mark. He moved his hand under the covers and slipped his hand underneath her pajama shirt, cupped her boob and squeezed lightly.

She let out a small moan, causing Mike to smirk lightly against her neck. She slapped his hand away and moved away from him. "Not now, Mike. I'm tired." She said softly.

Mike chuckled then kissed behind her ears. "C'mon, Sam." He moaned softly against her ear. "It's been weeks."

"It's been weeks because of you." She said, sitting up, fully awake now.

Mike could feel his boner going down and sighed. Well, he had no one to blame but himself, he had woken up the sleeping bear after all.

"Please don't start. It's 3 in the morning."

"And I'm sure you came in here at midnight from God-knows-where, doing God-knows-what with God-knows-who!" Sam said, facing her husband. She had waited up for him till midnight then decided it was no longer worth it and went to bed. Now he woke her up to have sex? Where did he get the nerve to do that?

"I was working, you know this!"

"Till midnight?" She scoffed at him, rolling her eyes. Oldest excuse in the book.

"Yes till midnight, it's not my fault that I've had to make more deliveries these past few weeks and besides the overtime gives me better pay, don't you want that?"

"What I want is my husband besides me during the dark hours of the day. What I want is a warm body to hold on to at night. What I want is someone to make me feel good." She said, her voice getting louder with each sentence.

"I can do that," he said, moving closer to her, "I can make you feel good."

He leaned closer and pressed a kiss to her lips softly at first and then harder. Sam gave in at first but then moved away. "Mike..." she started but he pressed his lips to hers again before she could contest once again.

Sam sighed and leaned into the kiss. Mike could feel his boner rising again and he slipped his hands underneath her shirt like he did earlier. This time she didn't contest it, instead she leaned back into the bed and let Mike do what he wanted.

Mike was excited and he moved quickly, taking off her shirt and then his. He cupped her breasts in his hands, alternating between light and hard squeezes. He brought his lips down from her lips to her nipple and took the left one in his mouth while his fingers played with the one on the right. He couldn't remember the last time he had her tits in her mouth and he wanted to take full advantage.

His tongue circled her nipple, earning light sighs from his wife. He sucked on it with vigor, his excitement only increasing. Sam wrapped her hands around her husband, getting into the swing of things. She arched her back, giving Mike more access to what he wanted.

The rest of their clothes melted away and Mike hurriedly searched through his wallet for a condom. He only had a small window of time before he completely lost his boner so he needed to find it fast. Sam rolled her eyes and grabbed him by his dick, bringing it close to her entrance.

"Forget the condom, we're no teenagers." She said, her voice seductive. Mike couldn't remember when his wife was so brazen and it wasn't like he didn't like it anyway. He reared his hips back and with a thrust, buried himself into his wife.

He groaned, feeling her pulsate around him. He thrusted into her quickly, propped up on his arms and gazing down at her heaving breasts. Sam's eyes were closed; she was concentrating, tightening the walls of her vagina so she could reach climax quickly with what little pleasure she was getting out of this.

Mike was having the time of his life, thrusting faster and faster. He placed his full body weight on Sam, who wrapped her legs around him. This created a tighter sensation around Mike that made Mike lose control. With a long groan and one last mighty thrust, he emptied himself into his wife.

He lay on top of her for a couple of seconds, still reeling from the intensity of his orgasm. He let out a breath then propped himself up on his hands, gazing down at the aftermath of what just happened. Sam had cum leaking out of her and her entire vulva was red.

"I'm sorry," Mike started, "I couldn't control it."

"It's fine. Anything up there waiting to be fertilized is way past its sell by date." Sam joked, throwing her legs off the edge of the bed and getting up.

Mike smiled. "Well that makes me feel a little better but I actually meant..."

"Don't worry about it, Mike. You know it takes me longer these days." Sam said good-naturedly, searching the bedside drawer for her vibrator. It didn't take her long to get there, in fact she could cum very quickly if she put her mind to it. But what good would it do if she made her husband feel guilty for not satisfying her? It was much easier to just finish up in the bathroom.

She grabbed the vibrator out of her nightstand, making sure to keep it out of Mike's sight. "I'm going to go clean up in the bathroom."

she announced, walking away quickly so Mike wouldn't suspect anything.

When she closed the bathroom door behind her, Mike could hear the faint steady rhythm of vibration coming from it. He sighed and turned over in bed. He appreciated his wife for not making him feel guilty about it but it was a little emasculating to hear evidence of a toy bringing her to completion in a way that he couldn't.

After a few minutes, he heard a soft cry come from the bathroom signifying that his wife had reached orgasm. He waited for a few seconds then heard the classic flush meant to disguise what she had just spent the last few minutes doing in there.

When Sam came out and saw her husband had his back to the bathroom door, she breathed a sigh of relief, it would be easier this way to hide the vibrator. She walked over to her side of the bed, hid the vibrator in the drawer of the nightstand that had a lock, placed her phone on the top of the nightstand and closed her eyes, ready to drift off to sleep.

She found slumber that night but Mike couldn't sleep, haunted by the faint sound of her vibrator and the humiliating fact that he could not satisfy his wife.

CHAPTER TWO: Endless Worries

Mike woke up the next morning and went to work with the sound and guilt still eating at him. He was on the road, at the helm of the delivery truck, trying to get some packages to a warehouse and all he could think about was his sex life in his marriage.

Last night was the first time in weeks that he had sex with his wife. He was attracted to her, he loved her but sometimes it felt like he was having sex with someone who was barely there. Last night just seemed to drive that statement in, she seemed into it at first but not enough to orgasm? He felt like something was lacking and if he could feel it then she probably felt it too.

But she hadn't said anything yet so perhaps he was only overthinking things. Just because his performance had been a little lack-luster last night didn't mean he couldn't get better or that their sex life was crumbling.

He shook his head and resolved to stop thinking about it. Instead of spending his time injecting negativity into his marriage, he could work on it. And that would involve getting back on time for once and trying to satisfy his wife as best he could tonight.

When he got back into the house later that night, he found his wife sleeping in bed. He glanced at his watch, 10:45 pm. Well that got rid of any ides of her cheating on him, she really did spend her nights waiting up for him which made him feel even more guilty.

He watched her sleep, taking in the beauty that was his wife. Even at 43, she was still the most beautiful woman he had ever met and he loved her just as much as he did as a 30 year old man when he married her 15 years ago.

It bothered him to think that something might be wrong with them, with him. It was getting harder to, well, stay hard and he couldn't last as long as he did when he was younger but he tried didn't he, to please her? He always gave it his best shot but it seemed his best was no longer cutting it.

His eyes fell on Sam's phone resting on the nightstand and he grew curious. She had it on her when she went to the bathroom last night, probably using it to watch or read something smutty. If he went through it, it would give him an idea of what she liked. Understanding her desires would help him fulfill them after all.

Not thinking beyond that, he took her phone off the nightstand and debated whether or not to unlock it. He had her passcode but she hadn't given it to him so he could snoop. With a deep sigh, and shutting down the guilt he felt in his chest, he entered her passcode and began scrolling through her phone.

He didn't find anything in her search history which made sense. If she was searching for something inappropriate, she wouldn't leave the evidence lying around. He decided to navigate to her social media instead, there were all those porn pages online, maybe she went there to look for something to watch.

His search landed him in a forum that he did not expect, "BBC fantasies." His pulse quickened and he tapped the thread.

The screen filled with images of big, tall black men railing older white women. He watched as video upon video of white women cheating on their partners with "BBC" came onto the page. He felt even more inadequate but strangely aroused when he watched a video of a black man fucking the shit out of someone's wife while he watched in the corner. There were stories of women escaping in the night while their husbands or boyfriends were asleep, seeking big black cocks that could satisfy them in a way that their partners could not.

It looked like Sam had been on this thread for months, watching these videos and reading these stories. Was this what she wanted? Is this what it took for her to cum nowadays, this and a vibrator apparently. A chill went through him, was she cheating on him after all?

Mike set the phone down, his mind racing. He could feel jealousy rising in him but there was another feeling as well. He looked down and sure enough, he was sporting a boner. Even if he felt inadequate he had to admit, the idea that Sam had been with someone else made him excited, but why?

This was clearly something she craved, something she wanted but what if she had already gotten it? What would he do if he found out that she hadn't been loyal to him?

Sam stirred in bed and opened her eyes slowly. She sat up in surprise. "You're home?" She quickly glanced at her bedside clock. "It's only 11pm."

"I know. I wanted to surprise you." He said, smiling.

Sam was confused but happy to see that her husband was in the house at this time for once. "Do you want to come to bed?"

Mike wasn't sure. He did have a boner he would like to take care of but he had so many conflicting feelings.

"We need to talk about something first."

Sam's brows furrowed in concern but Mike attempted to reassure her with a smile. "Is everything okay? Oh my goodness, were you fired? Is that why you're home?"

"I found the threads Sam."

Sam looked at him with confusion in her eyes but then recognition came into them. "Oh my goodness." She said, burying her face in her hands.

"Look Mike, I know you have a lot of questions…"

Mike raised his hand to cut her off. "I just have one honestly, are you cheating on me?"

Sam opened her eyes wide. "No no no! Of course not, I would never. I love you."

Mike looked into her eyes and in that moment, he believed her. He felt reassured now which brought him to his next question.

"When did this start? Is this something you want to do?"

"I don't know." She said, lifting her face out of her hands. "I honestly don't know. The whole thing was harmless at first, I was searching online for some porn to get me off and then I found this one video that made me feel...things."

"Things you don't feel with me?" Mike asked. That came out harsher than he wanted it to but he had to know.

Sam didn't say anything for some time and then she sighed. "Mike, I love you but you know that things haven't been the best...in that area. You're never home and when you are, we barely have sex. When we do have sex, I have to finish off in the bathroom because..."

"Because I don't make you cum? Is that it?"

"I think it's more than that if I'm being honest. We never try anything new, I mean it's been 15 years and we haven't even tried out a new position. I've seen women who look like me getting bent in ways that I didn't even know were possible and I have to admit, the thought of being those women, of being fucked by some of those men…well, it gets me there."

"I think I understand that but I don't know. Do you want to do that?" Mike asked, looking at his wife and studying her reaction.

"I would never cheat on you." Sam said, resolutely.

"Yeah but I can't expect you to keep running off to the bathroom to finish up every time we have sex. It's emasculating. I get all the satisfaction I could want from you."

Sam scoffed.

"What's that for?"

"You know that's not true. You're a man so it's easy for you to get there but I know that you know our sex life isn't the best. You're telling me that I'm always what you think about when you're getting off by yourself?"

Mike couldn't say anything but he knew she was right. They were spending less and less time together and even when they were, he wasn't exactly thinking about her if he wanted to climax. But somehow this was different, some of those threads featured people who actively wanted to step out of their marriages and that wasn't something that he wanted to do.

But then he thought about the ones he saw where the husband sat and watched his wife doing it with another man and he felt the boner start to rise again. Maybe that was something he wanted to do.

"If you had the chance to do this, have sex with a bbc, would you take it?" He asked her.

"Not if it upset you." Sam responded.

"What if it didn't? And what if I wanted to watch?"

Sam moved closer to her husband and held his hand. "What are you saying"

"I'm saying, I want us to do this. Let's find someone and make this fantasy a reality."

CHAPTER THREE: Unveiling Fantasies

"Are you sure about this?" Sam asked, the doubt creeping into her voice. She had gotten excited when Mike proposed the both of them working through this fantasy together but now she wasn't sure.

"Wouldn't it be less extreme to just search new positions online and try them out?" She asked.

Mike was already super into this idea and he knew that his wife was too but he didn't need her backing out now. He needed her to stay on board this train.

He squeezed her hand reassuringly. "Yes I am and you are too. We are doing this together."

A laptop hummed between them, the screen displaying a popular dating site for people looking for big black cocks. The both of them felt nervous but excited at the same time.

"How did you even find this place anyway?" Sam asked.

"I just had to search it up and I've seen reviews on it, it seems decent."

"Looking to date, romance or have sex with a hot, young black stud well this is where to meet them! These handsome young singles are looking to satisfy you in every way you want." the site read.

They went through the sign-up process together, they could sign up for a joint profile so they did. Sam selected a decent photo of the two of them and they crafted out their bio to show what they were looking for.

"Adventurous, loving couple looking for a respectful and confident young man to join us. Must be understanding, respectful of boundaries and ready to explore new things. Discretion is a must." their profile read.

"That looks okay, doesn't it?" Sam asked, looking to her husband for approval.

He nodded. "That's right. Now all we need to do is wait for people to sign up and then we can go through them together and talk to the ones we like."

"What does this mean for you though? Is this like a threesome kind of thing?" Sam asked. She knew what she wanted but what did her husband want out of the whole thing?

"Threesome? Oh no, I'm fine with watching, excited by the thought of it actually." Mike said. "Let's just talk to the guys and we'll move from there okay?"

Within hours of creating their profile, messages began flooding in. Over the next few days, Sam would sift through all the responses while Mike was at work and when he came back, they would check through the profiles together. Some of the messages were polite, other ones were explicit with the men just sending pictures of their junk and others were downright strange, describing all the weird things they wanted to do with both Mike and Sam.

The ones they liked, they set up video calls with. The first guy was a polite young man in his mid-twenties but he couldn't stop talking about himself. Sam thought that someone who was that self-involved wouldn't be much of a giver in the bedroom.

The second guy that they interviewed was a handsome man that seemed perfect at first but then all of a sudden he started listing out all of the demands he wanted from Sam. The both of them grew uncomfortable and ended the call quickly not wanting to get involved with someone like that.

The third guy was very attractive but he was overly flirtatious and seemed more interested in the idea of hooking up with Mike than Sam and this was more for her than him.

After more interviews like that, they began to feel disheartened. That was until they connected with Jay.

Jay seemed perfect and stood out as soon as they connected with him over the computer. He was a well-spoken man, confident and very respectful, putting them at ease almost immediately. He was in his early thirties and gave off a natural charisma that immediately drew them in.

"Hi Jay," Sam started, sounding instantly relieved by how charismatic this man seemed. "It's really lovely to meet you."

"Nice to meet you too." He replied with a warm smile. "I'm happy the both of you set this up, I was hoping to get to know your expectations before we got into anything?"

Sam and Mike looked at each other, pretty sure that they had just found their guy. As they kept talking, it became clear that Jay was everything they were looking for. He wasn't crass, he seemed interested in their desires and asked thoughtful questions. He didn't feel like someone storming into their marriage, he felt like he wanted to be a willing participant.

"We are loving this but do you mind if we set up a meeting in real life. We just want to see how this energy comes off in person." Mike asked.

Jay smiled warmly. "Of course. Just name the time and the place, I'll be there."

They set up a meeting with Jay at a nearby bar. Mike and Sam were pleased to find out they weren't being catfished when Jay came walking through the bar doors. They were a little worried that maybe the computer had warped his face or something but no, he looked just as handsome as he did on that video call.

Jay was a striking man, 6 foot 2, muscular, broad shoulders and smooth dark skin. He had short-cropped hair, a neat trimmed beard and Mike and Sam watched as his brown eyes searched for them in the crowd. He was wearing a tight, snug white shirt and his smile was inviting.

He found them sitting by the bar and walked over to them. He flashed a smile at Sam. "You look stunning." He said, giving her a lingering look.

"You don't look too bad yourself." She responded.

"It's nice to meet you two in person. You seem different from most people you find on sites like that." He said, shaking Mike's hand and giving Sam a polite hug.

"Different? In what way?" Mike asked.

"Like you're looking for something more, some people would have asked for a dick pic but you set up interviews."

"We love each other and things had been lacking so my husband decided he would let me go out there and experience one of my greatest fantasies…"

"A BBC? Classic." Jay said, chuckling slightly.

"We don't mean anything by it…" Mike interjected, hoping they weren't being offensive in some way.

"You're good, I find it flattering. And I have to admit, I'd be honored if you ended up choosing me."

"Oh we're well on our way there, we just need to know what you're all about." Sam asked.

"What do you mean?"

"Well you seem a little too good to be true. Why is a guy like you on a site like that?"

Jay chuckled then raised his hands to signal to the bartender. "Three beers please." He said before turning to the couple once again.

"I'm a man with very specific skills," He said, his voice velvety, leaning closer to the both of them, "and I like to use those skills on people who are very deserving."

Sam could feel heat start to spread all over her body, pooling between her legs. Something about this man was drawing her in and her mind was already full of dirty thoughts involving him bending her over and driving into her over and over.

Their beers came and Jay reached out to take a sip out the glass. Sam watched the foam from the beer stick to his mustache and the way he used his tongue to wipe it away. The heat between her legs turned into throbbing and she couldn't wait for them to skip this whole interview and get right to business.

"So tell me what are your boundaries?" Jay asked.

Sam glanced at Mike, who nodded in encouragement. "We just want to make sure everything is consensual and there's lots of communication involved. Mike will be present and...involved." She said the last word with as much innuendo she could muster.

"So he'll watch?" Jay asked, raising an eyebrow.

Mike nodded. "We want to make sure there's mutual respect and understanding in all of this."

"Of course, those are my top priorities as well. I'm sure this can be a positive experience for all of us. So are we doing this?"

Sam looked at Mike and he looked right back at her. They knew the answer to that, they had found their guy. They nodded at Jay together, who clapped.

"Great. So let's pound back a couple of beers and get this started shall we?"

CHAPTER FOUR: Surrounding Control

A couple of beers later, Mike had to go use the bathroom and that was when Jay made his move. He studied her face then came closer to her, leaning over till his mouth practically grazed her lips.

"You seem so wound up, a couple minutes with me and I bet I could make you come...loose." He said in a low voice that gave her butterflies. He leaned back and looked directly into her eyes, waiting for her reaction.

Sam swallowed and looked away, unable to meet his gaze. The moment suddenly felt charged and she knew what she wanted now, she wanted this man to take her.

She grabbed her beer and pounded it back, needing it to loosen her tongue. When she felt the rush from the alcohol passing through her, she looked at him and whispered, "What's it going to take to get a few minutes with you?"

He chuckled, loving her newfound boldness. "I don't need anything from you little miss, just your body. I have a hotel room not too far from here. If you and your husband are interested, we could go over there and I could...ravish you."

Mike appeared from the bathroom and saw his wife getting close with this man. He was supposed to be feeling jealous but instead all he could feel was excitement, excitement that only grew when Sam suggested going to Jay's hotel room.

He hadn't expected that things would go this fast and while they were on their way there in Jay's car, he still could hardly believe it but it all became real when they walked into his room and he shut the door behind them.

"The both of you are okay with anything that happens in this room?" Jay asked, moving closer to Sam as he said this.

Sam and Mike nodded in unison and Jay made his move. He took Sam into his arms and pressed a kiss to her lips. At first it was soft, getting her comfortable, teasing her before fully claiming it like it was his from the start.

Sam meets his kiss with a surprising hunger, desperate to quench that fire that had built between her legs. All Mike could do was watch from the corner as another man, a bigger man, a darker man, ran his hands all over his wife. He should feel jealous, tear him off her but all he felt was a raging boner growing in his pants at the sight.

Jay pulled away from Sam, his eyes glassy, aroused. Sam was an attractive woman, that was one of the things he noticed about her when he saw their joint profile. Blonde, blue eyes, shapely with wide hips and a lovely set of breasts. He didn't know what was going on with her and her husband but he was determined to show that body all the love it needed.

Jay couldn't hold himself out and grabbed her again, pushing her up against the wall and grinding his erection against her. His hands stroked her skin, his lips found her neck and he sucked at it intensely, earning a soft moan from Sam. He heard movement from the corner Mike was in and out of the corner of his eye, saw him take out his phone. Good, let him record so he could learn just the right way to treat a woman like this.

"I need to fuck you." Jay frowned against her neck. Sam was taken aback by such language. It was so vulgar, so laden with desire. When was the last time someone had made her feel this wanted, when was the last time someone had made it so clear that they needed her body.

Sam could smell the beer on his breath as he claimed her lips once again, that coupled with his touch made for a heady combination that intoxicated her. His left hand cupped her face while the right undid all the buttons on her shirt, revealing her white bra that could be unclasped from the front. He did that, letting her breasts out of their lacy cage.

A finger grazed her nipple lightly then his mouth followed shortly after. Sam threw her head back as she felt the heat and wetness from his mouth on her nipples. His tongue swirled her nipple and he sucked on it, sending pleasure radiating through Sam.

She rubbed herself against him, the fire down there rising even more. Taking the cue, he slipped his hands into the waistband of her jeans, his mouth still working wonders on her nipples. His hands head directly for her clit and he strokes it lightly. Sam could feel an orgasm start to build and she was so ready to let go, this would be the first time she came without a vibrator.

Jay slipped a finger into Sam, smirking against her nipple slightly. She let out a moan, feeling the pressure building in her. He moved his finger faster and faster while she bucked her hips against them, causing more pleasure to build until Sam felt she would come undone.

"Cum for me, you can do it." He whispered into her ears, moving his fingers within her faster. Sam's breathing got louder until she felt herself let go, cumming all over his fingers. Her knees get weak and Jay has to hold her up with his strength. She hadn't felt that much pleasure in such a long time and she felt on top of the world.

"I'm not done with you yet." Jay said, smiling at her. He looked in Mike's direction who was sporting a boner. "You still recording?" He asked.

Mike put the phone down. "I'm sorry, I just couldn't resist."

"You're good, keep recording. I want you to go back and see exactly how to please your wife."

"I'm not done with you yet." He said, pushing Sam towards the bed. He took off the rest of her clothes then his shirt and out of the pocket of his jeans, he took out a small square.

He took off his jeans, then his boxers and his dick springs up in front of Sam who can only look at it in awe.

"I-I don't think that will fit." She said, genuinely worried.

"You'll be fine, trust me" He walked over and leaned over. Feeling emboldened, Sam grabbed his length causing him to gasp. She stroked him and he closed. his eyes, letting himself embrace the pleasure.

He brought the condom packet he had taken out of his pocket and tore it open, slipping it on. He climbed on top of her then claimed her mouth once again. He pulled her legs apart and then positioned his dick in her entrance.

"If it gets overwhelming then just let me know." He said, before sliding into her slowly, closing his eyes in pleasure.

Mike watched as Jay climbed on top of his wife, getting ready to penetrate her. He could see the expression on her face, she was excited to receive him, excited to have him in her. A part of him had felt jealous when he watched Jay make his wife orgasm, something he hadn't been able to do in a long time but he couldn't ignore the other feeling; the one of anticipation. He wanted his wife to get fucked by this man.

Seeing Sam so eager to receive a dick that was much bigger than his made him feel a kind of excitement that he hadn't felt before. He got his phone ready and took a seat on a chair nearby, he was going to record everything that happened today.

CHAPTER FIVE: Coital Bliss

The phone's camera in Mike's zoomed in on the place where Jay and Sam were connected. Jay was asking slow, gentle thrusts into Sam to get her used to him while Mike worked the camera, struggling with how much the sight turned him on.

He couldn't take it any longer, he had to touch himself. He passed the camera into his non-dominant hand while he unzipped his pants with his dominant one. He took out his dick, only half the size of Jay's and started stroking it to the sounds Sam was making whilst under Jay, to the sound of his skin slapping against hers.
He imagines it was him for a second, making his wife make those loud moans but that thought didn't turn him on half as much as watching Jay and Sam did. Sam was holding onto him for dear life whilst Jay went in and out of her in a steady, firm rhythm. How could Sam handle all of that?

"You like that?" Jay sighed into Sam's ear. Sam loved it, every thrust into her felt like a thousand stars were exploding in parts of her she didn't even know existed. She grabbed his waist, not wanting him to stop and pulled him deeper into her, she wanted him to fill her completely.

Jay groaned and sank into her, increasing the force of his thrusts. If this woman wanted more of him, he would give her more. "Fuck," he murmured against her neck, feeling himself getting closer and closer. He hadn't expected her to feel this good, he couldn't believe a pussy this good had wasted on that man for years. That didn't matter now though, because he was going to show it and her all the love it deserved.

He went faster, causing Sam to cry out. He leaned over and whispered into her ear, "Come for me, you can do it. Fuck, you feel so fucking good." He punctuated each word with a thrust, letting the sensation run through him. "I'm so close." He groaned.

Sam couldn't believe that she was making such a man feel these things, did she really drive this man that crazy? Was this all just part of the experience he was used to providing or was this something more. She couldn't figure it out, all she knew in that moment was this man wanted her and couldn't get enough of her. He was driving himself into her, over and over again because he needed her and that was enough to make her come undone.

She let out a long, drawn out sigh as wave after wave of pleasure washed over her. Nothing had made her feel like this before, not her husband, not even her vibrator. She buckled and shook underneath Jay holding unto him for dear life while he went to town on her, free to pound away into her as hard as he could now that he had gotten her to come.

"Fuck, fuck, uhhhh." He groaned, the muscles in his arms growing taut. Sam could feel his dick pulsating in her as he came. In the corner, Mike was stroking his dick furiously, incredibly aroused by everything he had just seen, he had no idea his wife was capable of making such sounds. He came into his hands, his own groan washed out by the sounds Jay was making.

He looked down at the mess he had made, cum all over his hands and his pants. He looked up at Jay who had taken his wife's lips once again, he saw the way Sam held on to Jay like he was her lifeline and he felt his dick twitch to life once again, this was an incredibly hot scene.

Jay stood up and went to the bathroom, coming back with some wipes for Sam. He took the time to clean her up before heading back to clean himself up as well. When he came back, he found Mike on the bed beside his wife, red in the face from stroking himself. Sam was back in her clothes, her hair tousled from their encounter, looking the picture of post-coital bliss.

"So," he started, taking his pants off the ground and putting them back on. "How would you rate your first BBC experience?" He threw this question at Sam whose eyes lit up immediately.

"Ten out of ten!" She exclaimed. "I didn't even know I could-"

"Scream like a banshee in bed?" Jay said, chuckling. "I told you all I needed was a couple of minutes with you. And you, Mike? How do you feel?"

"I feel...surprisingly good. I think you may have taught this old dog some new tricks even." He said, smiling widely. He reached out and took his wife's hand who squeezed it.

"Thank you for being open to this, Mike." Sam said, placing a chaste kiss on her husband's forehead. "I don't know a lot of men who would be okay with their wives..." she trailed off, as her mind went back to all the dirty things that Jay had done to her.

Jay chuckled to himself. He had to admit, in all his years of providing these kinds of services to disgruntled white couples, this was the most unique one he had ever encountered. And Sam? She didn't see like a woman who wanted to stick it to her husband, she looked like someone who had a lot of love to give and that made Jay intrigued.

He dug into the pockets of his pants and brought out his card. "If you ever need me or my services, or if you're ever in the mood for a beer and a good conversation, call me." He said, handing the card over to Mike and Sam.

"So does this mean that we'll see you again?" Sam asked, as she and Mike stood up to head to the door.

"Of course you'll see me again." Jay said, grabbing Sam and kissing her deeply once again. He smacked her ass as she walked away, causing her to get red in the face. "No way I'm letting a nice piece of ass like this go to waste."

Sam and Mike made their way back to the bar where they met Jay, their car still in the parking lot. When they got home, all they could think about was what happened at Jay's hotel room.

"How much did you record?" Sam asked.

"Everything." Mike said, taking out his phone and showing her the footage. Sam could feel throbbing down there all over again as she visually relived all of the things that Jay had done to her back at the hotel.

"Seeing everything from that perspective. It's all so...dirty." Sam said. "Did I ever sound like that when I was with you?"

"Not even close." Mike said, laughing even though he really should feel jealous. "I think the last time I heard your scream like that was maybe when we first got married."

Sam chuckled. "Yeah, you definitely knew a few tricks back then." The smile from her face fell. "Is it bad that I want to do it again? Feel those things again?"

Mike shook his head. "Is it bad that I want to watch you do it again?"

"No it's not but it's just...what if I become addicted to it or something? What if I don't want to stop or the only thing that can make me cum is a big black cock?"

"Well then," Mike started. "I better start getting used to seeing more of Jay around."

CHAPTER SIX: A New Identity

Sam found herself alone in her living room, her fingers hovering over the keyboard of the laptop in front of her. It was a weekday so of course, Mike had left her all alone to go to work. On other days, she would lament her lack of employment but not today. Today, she was lurking on a hot wives community forum, reading up on stories similar to hers.

She had known that there was a name for women like her, women who were open to being sexual with other men outside of their husbands and like her husband, some of the partners of these women liked to watch the sexual encounters as well. Sam wasn't sure if she wanted to sleep with other men outside of Jay but she did know that after her first session with him, she was excited by the idea.

She took a deep breath, she had been wondering if she could share her story. She felt like she needed to talk about this with someone other than her husband and she didn't have any other girlfriends so this was the only other option. Her fingers hesitated over the keyboard then she started typing, recounting her night with Jay and everything that came with it.

"A couple of days ago, I had my first experience with a black bull. For context, I'm a 43 year old white woman who has been married for 15 years. I love my husband but things have been a bit dull in the sack lately. I had been lurking on some forums like this and my husband

found out then let me have sex outside our marriage on the condition that he watched.

It was the most incredible, intense and most liberating time of my life. He absolutely dominated me and made me feel things that I have never felt before. My husband is fully supportive and I even feel more connected to him but I don't know what this means for us now. Is this a one time thing because I don't want it to be, I like the idea of getting railed by a big dick but I don't know how long my husband can be comfortable with it. Anyway, I just wanted to share my story."

Sam hit "post" then watched as the words that she wrote went live on the forum. She wasn't sure how long it would take for people to respond but she was surprised to find the notifications pouring in almost immediately. She clicked through the first replies, all of them supportive.

"I just had my first bull too, best time of my life!"
"My husband loves to watch me get railed by a thick bull too, love that for you!"
"It sounds like you had an amazing experience. Don't stop exploring."
"You know what they say! 'When you go black, you can't go back!"

There was one that really stood out to her though. One that seemed to understand the confusion that she was feeling right now.

"Hi there! I was in a similar position a while back as well, married long term but lacking in the bedroom. I tried everything to bring the spice back, not just in our sex life but in our love life as well until I decided to take matters into my own hands and fuck someone more

endowed than my husband. I didn't care if my husband was involved or not, I had tried to heighten our sex life but it wasn't taking so I decided to be a little selfish. Eventually though, he started watching and we've never been happier. My advice would be to not overthink this, think about your own satisfaction. You're not too old to enjoy sex and if you've found a way to have it in a more fulfilling way then go for it. Take the bull by the horns girl!"

This anonymous commenter filled her heart with warmth. She had read through every single comment, soaking in the encouragement from the community but this particular one spoke to her. How many times had she tried to awaken the spark in her life with Mike? She loved her husband but things had been so mundane for a long time. She had finally found something to make her feel good, in a way that she deserved so she was going to embrace it. Mike would just have to get on board.

Motivated by the supportive comments from the rest of the hot wives community she decided to have a conversation with her husband when she came back home.

When Mike came back, Sam was ready to be completely honest. She wanted the both of them to have an open conversation about Jay and how this would affect them moving forward.

Mike walked into their bedroom and kissed Sam on her cheek. "Hey honey, I hope you weren't too lonely at home today?"

Sam watched as her husband took off his work clothes and took in his body. He was no stud like Jay but he had his charm. She had no intention of leaving their marriage but maybe there was a version of their marriage that had Jay in it and any other man she would be interested in.

"I actually wasn't lonely, I spent most of the day online reading up on other women like me."

"Other women like you?" Mike asked, raising an eyebrow. What was this about?

"Other women who have been with men outside their marriage. I posted about our experience on the 'hot wives' forum and I got a lot of support. It also made me realize something."

Mike said felt anxiety wash over him. What was she trying to say? Was Sam trying to tell him that she was no longer interested in their relationship? He had thought this whole thing with Jay may have been a one time thing like having a threesome when your relationship got too boring but what if it made her realize that she could do so much better than him.

"Please don't leave me." He blurted out.

"What?!" Sam exclaimed. "What do you mean? I don't want to leave you!"

Mike blinked in surprise. "You don't?"

"Of course not, I love you."

"But things have been so lackluster lately." Mike said. What was he saying? His wife had just told him that she wanted to stay so why was he looking for excuses for her?

"Of course they have been, we've been married for 15 years, things would get a little monotonous but what I realized wasn't that I want to leave you."

"So what did you realize?" Mike asked.

"I realized that I don't want to stop this thing we've started. I really enjoyed that first time with Jay and I want to do it again and maybe not even just with Jay, maybe with other men as well." She said, reaching for his hand and squeezing it.

Mike raised his eyebrows slightly but he didn't pull away. "You want to sleep with other men?"

"Yes," Sam admitted, her voice not even shaking. "It's really exciting and I want to take charge of my sex life in this way, it's fulfilling in a way that I didn't expect. I think this is something that I need to do for myself and I want to know if you would be okay with that."

Mike went silent for some time, trying to process her words. She didn't want to leave him but she did want to step out of their marriage. How did he feel about that? He knew how he was supposed to feel; angry, jealous and maybe even a little disgusted by the proposal but then he thought back to the time he watched Jay fuck his wife, how aroused he was by the fact and he knew what he wanted to say.

"Sam, I have to admit, it was a little strange watching you sleep with Jay but then it really turned me on. I loved watching you experience that much pleasure, it made me happy seeing you so fulfilled."

"Wait, so you're not upset or jealous?"

Mike shook his head. "No, I'm not. It's unconventional but I can definitely see you doing that again, I only hope you can let me watch it every now and again. I don't think I've ever come as much as I did that day."

"Oh! Thank you, thank you, thank you! Your support means everything to me." She said, bringing her husband close and hugging him tight.

He smiled, hugging her back. "I trust you Sam and if you want to explore this further, you have my full support and permission."

"I do want that and I was hoping you'd let me invite Jay over when you're out working tomorrow?" She said, her voice hopeful that he would agree.

"Of course, I just need you to do one favor."

"And what's that?" Sam asked, curious.

"Record it for me. I want to watch it later."

CHAPTER SEVEN: Mingling Desires

Sam was feeling good after her conversation with her husband the other day but it still took her some time before she felt brave enough to reach out to Jay. She felt a burning desire to see him again and have him explore her body all over again but she hesitated every time she reached for her phone to call the number on his card.

It wasn't until a week later that she finally swallowed all her anxiety and reached for her phone to text him, her fingers no longer trembling as they typed out the text.

"I've been thinking about our time together and I would love to see you again."

- Sam.

A response came almost immediately.

"I haven't been able to get you out of my mind. I'm glad you reached out, meet me at the bar we first hung out in an hour."

- Jay

Sam arrived first. She chose a corner table, one that was away from prying eyes and sat down to order, ordered a beer then waited in with bated breath and anticipation. Her drink came and she sipped it nervously, checking her phone for any sort of communication from Jay.

Finally, she saw him walk in, his presence commanding. Jay spotted her and smiled then waved, making his way over to her. Her pulse quickened as he walked over to her and took a seat across from her.

"Hey," Jay said, smiling at her. His voice was smoother and deep, and it brought back memories of when he was whispering sexy things into her ear while he was deep within her.

"Hi, Jay," she said, her voice coming out breathless and choked. "I have been looking forward to this. I've actually been really nervous leading up to this, I'm surprised you wanted to meet up at all." She was rambling and she hoped that didn't turn Jay off.

"Hey," he said, reaching out and taking her hands in his. He locked his eyes onto hers and she felt such a magnetic pull to him in that moment. "Don't overthink this, I had fun with you and I want to keep having fun with you. You look amazing by the way."

She smiled and tucked her a strand behind her ears, blushing. "Thank you, so do you."

They started chatting, Jay leaning in, his eyes never leaving hers. He seemed to be gazing right into her soul and it made her feel like she was the only person in the room.

"Do you mind if I ask you something?" She asked, suddenly.

"Sure you can, go ahead."

"Please don't take offense to this but you seem so put together. I just mean that out of all the guys that my husband and I saw on that site, you are the least sleazy. What made you sign up on a place like that?"

Jay chuckled and took a sip out of his beer that just arrived. "Everyone has their kinks and mine is making people's fantasies come true. I'm very particular about the kind of people I get involved with, you and your husband seemed genuine and I wanted to be involved in that."

"Besides," he said, his voice taking a more intimate tone, "It doesn't hurt that there's an attractive woman in the mix. It pains me to think that someone like you isn't getting all the fulfillment she needs. I want to fix that, I just need you to let me."

Sam felt heat rush to her cheeks, this man was very alluring. "And what if I want that, what if I want you to let you?"

"Then why don't we take this somewhere more private and I can show you all the wonders we can experience together."

Sam's breath hitched and her eyes widened. The way Jay was looking at her made her pulse quicken and that smile, that cocky smile, made her melt. "My husband isn't home, could we go to mine? My car's right outside."

Jay leaned back, his lips curling into a sexy smile and his eyes darkened with lust. "Lead the way, my lady."

The drive to her house was charged, she couldn't wait for what was coming. Her mind raced with thoughts of what was to come, her body hummed with excitement. She kept stealing glances at Jay, her hands gripping the wheel of the car tight as his hands roamed all over her thigh. Being around him was so intoxicating and she felt liberated in a way that she hadn't felt in a long time.

When they got to her house, Sam led her inside. She led him into her bedroom and sat on the bed while he towered over her. Jay stepped closer, cupping her cheek with his hand.

"Do you really want this?" he asked, his voice gentle and his eyes filled with desire.

Sam nodded, her eyes locking onto his. "Yes, I'm very sure."

Jay's lips curved into a sultry smile. "Then let's not waste any more time."

He leaned in to kiss her and she felt a rush of emotions run through her, the foremost of which was deep, burning desire.

"Oh wait, my husband asked me to record this for him. Is that okay? There's a camcorder in the bedside drawer and we can set it up."

"Yeah that's fine." He said, walking over to the drawer. He took out the camcorder and set it up on a shelf that stood opposite and in the direct sight of the bed. When he put it on, he walked over to her and pushed her into the bed.

"Let's get started then." He said, claiming her lips in a deep, passionate kiss.

Jay pushed a hand under her shirt and into her bra, freeing one breast. Like a flash, his mouth closed onto the nipple, sucking on it through the shirt. Sam felt a desire pool between her legs as his tongue made patterns all over. her sensitive nipples.

His hand slipped into her pants while another unzipped his pants. Sam was impatient so she tried to push his own pants down. Before she knew it, the both of them were naked and he was grinding his erection against her clit, making heR gasp in bliss.

He slipped his hard erection into her, and her eyes rolled back as her body embraced him. He hissed as he buried himself in her. "Yessss..." he groaned, his eyes glassy as he drove himself into her. He had only just entered her and he was already panting like he couldn't get enough of her or like he was close. Either way, it drove Sam to the brink of madness as she lay there in disbelief that she was bringing this man that much pleasure.

Feeling brazen, she rolled Jay off of her and got on top of her. She wanted him badly, so she straddled him. She could already imagine how his dick would feel when she slid down the length.

She raised her hips and took him inside of her, going down slowly, inch by him. His eyes rolled to the back of his head and he opened his mouth in a silent groan. She squeezed her muscle around him and slid down the rest of his length, taking him fully in.

She began to move up and down, Jay jerked his hips up to meet her, matching her thrust for thrust. It felt amazing and Sam could feel her own orgasm building in her. She couldn't remember the last time she had done this, it had been years. The last time she had ridden a man was during the early years of her marriage and now here she was, bouncing up and down another man's penis like she was a young cowgirl.

He gripped her hips and began to grind her against him. He tightened his jaw and let out a short, hoarse gasp as Sam went up and down and grinded her clit against him. She leaned forward and he took a nipple into his mouth. He rolled the nipple around in his mouth with his tongue, sucking on it like his life depended on it.

"I want you to bounce on this dick like you want to break it. Show that pretty pussy off to your husband, let him see how much you love taking this big dark cock in you, c'mon." He said, driving himself into her by bucking his hips.

Sam could feel the pressure building in her and she grinded down on him hard. That was all it took for her to come all over him. She let out a loud, long moan and collapsed on top of him, the muscle of her walls contracting all over Jay's dick.

Jay held on to her hips, pounding her as he sought his own release. He closed his eyes and his face contorted due to the ecstasy he was feeling. Sam could feel his dick pulsing in her as he gave one last, hard thrust and came in her. They weren't wearing a condom, and under normal circumstances she should be worried that another man was filling her with his seed but she couldn't care less. All she cared about was the way he throbbed in her, the sound of his groan and the way his hands gripped her hips tightly while he emptied himself into her.

He chuckled and raised her hips off slightly so her vagina was in full view of the camcorder. "I want your husband to see my cum dripping out of you." He said, as he watched his cum fall out of her and onto his body.

Sam laughed and rolled off him, letting herself come down from all the pleasure she had just experienced.

"That was..incredible." she said, sighing in post-coital bliss.

"Oh honey," he laughed, wrapping his arm around her and placing a soft kiss on her forehead. "That was only the beginning."

Jay looked at her intensely, so intensely it gave her butterflies. She was the farthest thing from a schoolgirl yet this man was able to make her feel like a teenager again.

"Why are you looking at me like that?" She asked him.

He hesitated, his eyes seemingly searching hers. He seemed to be weighing his next words carefully. "I think...I might want more."

Her eyes opened wide. "W-what does more mean?"

He sighed. "It means that I might be considering this arrangement. I don't know, I just get the sense that there's something here. Something more than just sex."

Sam sat up and used the sheets to cover herself. "You do realize I'm married right?"

"Yeah and you're fucking me? C'mon be for real, you wouldn't be with me if part of you wasn't over your husband."

Sam blinked rapidly, taken aback by his audacity. "I love my husband, I made that clear to you from the start."

"The both of you can say whatever makes you feel better about this but I've been here too many times and I know the truth. The sooner you accept it, the better. You and your husband may be on the last leg but we...we still have a shot."

Sam couldn't believe what she was hearing. She liked having sex with Jay, yes but that didn't give him the right to talk about her marriage in that way.

"I think you need to leave." She said, her tone firm.

Jay's eyebrows creased. "C'mon don't be like that." He said, reaching for her.

She dodged his touch and walked towards the door. "I told you at the beginning that you needed to respect my connection with my husband. I don't appreciate you insinuating I should leave him for you."

"So what? You're going to dump me?" Jay asked, looking a little sad by that prospect.

"I don't think this is going to work out, not if you're going to try to get in the way of me and my husband." Sam said.

Jay sighed and took his clothes off the floor, walking over to the door. He looked at her with a pained look in his eyes.

"You don't have to-"

Sam raised her hand to stop him from talking and he took the hint, walking away. When Sam was alone she walked over to her bed and buried her face in her hands.

Was this the last time she would ever see Jay?"

THE END BOOK 1

CHAPTER EIGHT: The Conversation

It had been a couple of days since Sam had kicked Jay out of her house. Since then, she had woken up everyday to calls, texts and emails from him asking for her to talk to him. She didn't want to entertain him anymore because she had the feeling that it was only going to be a matter of time before he overstepped boundaries again but she had to admit to herself that it was incredibly tempting.

Jay was a big part of her sexual awakening and it was hard to let someone who had been an integral part of that go. Sending him away was the right choice, she knew this but did this mean that she would have to go back to mundane sex with her husband?

She loved Mike, her heart would always belong to him but how could she go back to finishing herself off in the bathroom every time they had her after she had experienced some of the most intense orgasms of her life in the hands of Jay. When her thoughts went that way, it made her contemplate taking up her phone and reaching out to him again, this time with stronger boundaries.

But she knew that would be futile, what if a situation came where she was high on oxytocin and he manipulated her into leaving her husband for him. That was not a scenario that she wanted to entertain in the slightest.

It would only be a matter of time before he became possessive and that was energy that she wouldn't want in her marriage, not when Mike had been so understanding of her wants and needs.

After the last time they met, Mike had watched the video and had of course, found it very arousing. He had asked her when she and Jay would be meeting up again so he could be a part of their tryst this time but she had hesitated to answer him. When he pressed her, she had no choice but to come clean.

"I don't think we'll be seeing Jay anymore." She had said cryptically.

Mike had raised an eyebrow, curious. "Did something happen with you two? Oh my goodness did he disrespect you in some way? I'll kill him if he upset you." Mike had said, getting all protective.

Sam laughed. Mike was well into his 40s with back pain that made him take painkillers periodically. If he tries to go up against Jay, he would end up in the hospital. Still though, she appreciated his concern and liked that he was still willing to fight for her honor like they were kids again.

"No, he didn't do anything to me. Well, he didn't do anything that I didn't like anyway." Sam said, smiling to herself.

"So what's the problem?" Mike asked, raising his eyebrow once again.

"I'm just bored." Sam said, lying through her teeth. She didn't want to tell Mike the real reason that she had cut things off with Jay, she didn't want to get into it but she still had to give him something so he would get off her back.

"Bored? You've only been with him a couple of times, how could you be bored already?" Mike pressed.
"People can get bored Mike. It happens all the time, maybe I'm ready for something new, I don't know. I just know that I don't want to get involved with Jay anymore, can't you respect that?" Sam said, feigning anger. Maybe if she acted like she was upset, Mike would drop it.

Like she anticipated, Mike dropped the matter and didn't bring it up anymore after the day. That left Sam enough time to process everything that happened on her own time.

At the end of the day, she had realized that Jay's attitude was a red flag but that didn't mean that she didn't want to continue exploring this new side of herself. She hoped that Mike would be understanding when she told him everything that happened.

The next weekend that followed the day Sam kicked Jay out of her house, she got up early as she had spent the night before scrolling online forums for people who were perhaps in a similar situation as hers. People who wanted to enjoy other men, preferably BBCs but still wanted to preserve the relationships with her partners. She hadn't found much but that didn't deter her from wanting to keep searching.

She was making herself some coffee, contemplating everything that had happened when she heard the sound of footsteps. No doubt they were Mike's but they still made her tense.

He walked into the kitchen in a robe, rubbing his eyes as he made his way towards her. She smiled to herself, he was kind of cute even after all this time.

"Morning," Mike said to his wife as he walked into the kitchen. He grabbed a mug from the counter and poured himself some coffee. "You're up early."

Sam was leaning against the kitchen counter nursing a mug of coffee of her own. She had been thinking about the incident from the days before when she sent Jay out of her house after having incredible sex with him. It was great but she had an inkling that if she continued, her relationship with her husband would be undermined and that was something she did not want to deal with.

"Yeah, I couldn't sleep. I've been thinking about…stuff." She said cryptically.

Mike took a sip out of the mug in his hands then leaned against the counter beside her. "Let me guess, this is about Jay? You know, you never really told me what happened between you two. Based on the video I watched from the last time you hooked up with him, everything looked great."

"It was great still he basically told me that it was only a matter of time till I left you for him."

"He said that?" Mike asked, his brow furrowed.

"Yeah he did and I told him that wasn't going to be the case. It was just out of nowhere because when we started all this I thought we made it clear where we stood on the whole thing. The intention was to have a little fun, to explore and I thought he understood that."

Mike looked deep in thought, trying to process everything Sam had just said. He was a little conflicted; on the one hand he was happy that his wife stood up for them but on the other he was confused because what if she was denying a part of herself just to please him? What would she do if she couldn't act on this new fantasy of hers?

"So that's it then? No more Jay?" Mike said finally.

"I'm not sure honestly. This whole experience has been so...amazing. I don't want to stop exploring this but I don't want it to affect us in any way. I want to do it with someone who ends up like Jay who tries to manipulate me into being his alone. I'm looking for dick , not a new partner."

"I'm going to take that as a compliment," Mike said chuckling. "I guess I should be glad that you don't want to sacrifice us while you explore. Honestly it was one of my biggest fears when this whole thing started. What if that other guy steals her away from me, you know? But I feel better now having heard you explain how you feel."

"Of course, love. And I appreciate you being so understanding so far." Sam said, leaning over and giving her husband a small kiss on the cheek.

Mike smiled, cupping the part of his cheek that she had kissed. "You're welcome, you know I want you to feel free to explore. Anything that makes you happy."

"Yeah, but I don't know how to do that in a way that doesn't involve sacrifice."

Mike went into deep thought then set his mug down. "Maybe we need to find people like you."

"What do you mean?" Sam said, setting her own mug down.

"Maybe we're coming at this from the wrong angle. We've been looking for unattached men and that has the potential to get messy but maybe we need to get with people like us. It's less risky than going solo with random guys who can get possessive." Mike suggested.

"I'm not understanding, Mike."

"Look, I'm just saying there's got to be people like us out there. Maybe you can find a man who is like you and the both of you can do your thing."
Sam thought it over. "That's actually not a bad idea actually and it could be a way for us to keep things exciting. Would you be open to that?"

Mike wrapped his arms around her, pulling her close. "I'm open to it. How about this, let's just take it slow and figure this out together. No pressure. Let's go online and find out more then go from there?"

Sam nodded. "I like the sound of that."

CHAPTER NINE: The Invitation

Sam and Mike decided that the best place to start was online, so they spent the next few days doing research. On the hotwives forum where Sam posted her experiences when she started her journey, they posted what they were looking for and got a ton of suggestions from people who had been in that lifestyle for years.

"It sounds like you might be interested in swinging! Why don't you try this site? My husband and I found a couple that we are both so comfortable with and that we're all married makes us feel more secure about our connection."

"Swinging," Mike started, looking over Sam's shoulder at the computer in front of her, "that seems like a good start."

"What even is that?" Sam asked, looking at the computer with a confused expression on her face. "It feels like we're always coming across new terms all the time, it's hard to keep up."

Mike squinted at the computer screen then typed in the word 'swinging' in the search engine. "Says here it's when one or both partners engage in sexual activities with other people. Some people prefer to do it with other partnered people, oh like us! That's what we're looking for."

"I suppose that does sound like us." Sam said, feeling nerves coming on. This was all very overwhelming but there was an undercurrent of excitement in the midst of it all.

"There's a site where we can join, connect with other couples. Ready to give it a shot?" Mike asked, looking over at his wife.

Sam swallowed then nodded, no choice but to dive in.

The site was surprisingly enlightening for them. Not only was it a place to connect with other people, it also educated about the lifestyle with tips and cautionary tales to be mindful of. All over the site, it seemed to emphasize one thing; communication. Anyone who wanted to get involved in this had to keep their partner in the loop every step of the way.

"Communicate, that seems easy enough right?" Sam said, looking over to her husband.

Mike nodded. "I don't have anything to hide from you."

They registered themselves on the site, posting pictures of themselves, their interests and what they were into. After that, they added some information about themselves and logged off with the intention of signing back after a few days to check on their progress.

A couple of days later, they logged back in and went through the latest posts and some couples who had shown interest in their profiles. Just at that moment, a message popped up in their inbox from a couple named Andre and Leila.

"They seem friendly." Mike said, leaning closer to the screen. He read the message aloud as Sam wasn't with her glasses.

'Hi Sam and Mike, we noticed you're a little new to all of this so allow us to introduce ourselves. We're Andre and Leila, an interracial couple that lost meeting like-minded couples. We're hosting a private event this weekend and would love you to come through. It's a small gathering, just a few couples getting to know each other in an intimate environment. It might be the perfect introduction to this lifestyle. No pressure, just come through if you can. Looking forward to connecting!'

'This was it', Sam thought with excitement. This was the perfect way to get into the flow of things. "What do you think?"

"I think it sounds perfect. We can meet Andre and Leila as well as other couples like us. Let's do it."

The event was in two days and it came faster than the both of them expected. Before they knew it, they were driving up to the address that Andre and Leila had given them. It was a fancy neighborhood and that made Sam nervous and very aware of the fact that they were about to enter a space filled with complete strangers.

They pulled up to a sleek house at the end of a cul-de-sac and got out of the car. Sam took a deep breath, smoothing down her dress. She had spent a lot of time picking out her outfit - a body hugging black gown that made her feel really sexy but wasn't too revealing. She took her husband's hand and together, they walked up to the door of the house.

They knocked on the door and waited for a while before it was opened. The sound of the soft bass music hit them first before they took in the man that was in front of them. It was a tall, muscular man with high-top hair and a warm smile. He had dark skin and was wearing a tight white shirt that contrasted it. Sam recognized him immediately, he was Andre, the man who had invited her tonight.

"You must be Mike," he said, extending a handshake which Mike accepted. He turned to Sam and gave her a lingering, hungry look. "And you must be Sam, I'm glad you could make it out."

"Happy to be here and thank you for inviting us. I have to admit, I wasn't expecting such a handsome young man to be the host of this party." Sam said, taking a look inside to catch a glimpse of what was happening inside.

Andre laughed, a deep attractive sound. "Young? I haven't been young since I was in my thirties. But I appreciate the compliment. Please come in, let me introduce you to Leila and some of the people we know."

Sam and Mike stepped in, taking in the environment. They were led into a large living room where small groups of people were gathered with drinks in their hands. Some groups of people were making out, hands everywhere and in a little corner, an orgy was about to start.

Sam's eyes bulged. "I didn't know this was that kind of party."

"It's mostly a mixer but some people can't help themselves sometimes. You don't have to do anything you're not comfortable with but if you do feel like getting dirty, there's lube and condoms available. Now where's my wife, I want her to meet you two."

A petite woman approached them then wrapped her arms around Andre before giving him a small peck on his lips. "I've been looking everywhere for you, you left me alone to play host." The petite woman said, pulling away fro Andre and giving him a pouty face.

"I'm sorry, I had to get the door. Leila, I want you to meet Sam and Mike, they just arrived." Andre said, turning to face Sam and Mike.

"Oh yes, I recognize them! The cute couple from that site. I'm so glad you two could make it." Leila said, hugging Sam then Mike for a couple seconds too long.

Andre and Leila took them around the room, introducing them to other couples and placing some drinks in their hands. Mike and Sam started to relax and soon they were on a couch with Andre and Leila, slightly tipsy and heavily flirting.

Leila sat on Andre's thighs, her hands in his hair. Sam felt a little envy watching the two of them. They behaved like newly in love teenagers, handsy and jovial.

"If you don't mind me asking, how old are you two?" Sam said, blurting out the question before she could really think it through.

Andre and Leila looked at each other then burst into laughter. "I know we look a little young but please don't hold it against us." Andre said, his laughter settling into a light chuckle.

"I'm 45 years old and Leila here is 40."

Sam opened her eyes wide. "Wow, I wish I looked that good at 40."

Andre smirked and looked her over. "I don't know what you're talking about, you look really good right now. That dress is very...alluring." He said, his eyes lingering on her body.

Sam could feel heat creep onto her face and then she felt it start to creep downwards. Andre was a very attractive man, no doubt about that and he definitely had an effect on her.

The evening crept on and the atmosphere started to get a little more charged. The more people drank, the more loose they became and soon people began pairing off, leaning into each other and heavily making out. Andre and Leila didn't seem interested in what was happening around them, their eyes were completely focused on Sam and Mike.

Sam on the other hand was very interested in everything that was happening. She caught sight of a pair not too far from them, the woman was sitting in the man's lap and they were kissing deeply. Another couple was openly making out on the arm of the sofa near them.

"It's a lot, I know," Andre said, smiling slightly. "But it can be pretty fun."

"Do you guys always host sex parties?" Sam blurted out again, earning a laugh from Mike who was deep into his fifth beer.

Andre and Leila laughed again. "They weren't always sex parties, in a way they still aren't. We just saw a need for people to get together if they were interested in swinging or sharing partners and then we found that people also needed a safe space to do their thing. So we said, 'why not our place?' " Leila said.

"Do you ever get involved?" Mike asked.

"Only with people that we really like." Andre said, his voice dripping with innuendo. As he said that, Leila got off his thighs and sat beside Mike. Sam looked over at Andre and he beckoned her over. When she got closer to him, he made her sit on his lap in Leila's place then whispered in her ears, 'and we really like you.'

His hands crept up her thigh then under her dress. He leaned closer and kissed behind her ears, whispering softly in an alluring voice, "If I'm doing anything you're not comfortable with, let me know and I'll stop."

Sam swallowed as his hand continued creeping up her thigh whilst the other one cupped her neck. She turned her head and saw Mike and Leila watching them intently, clearly both aroused by what they were watching.

This was it, they were finally getting into the swing of things.

CHAPTER TEN: The Next Step

By now, Andre's hand had found what it was looking for, shifting Sam's panties and playing with her clit. Hr brought his mouth away from Sam's ear and to her neck, nibbling slightly then sucking while his hand worked its magic. Sam inhaled sharply as Andre moved his finger in circles over her clit and she could feel herself getting increasingly aroused.

Mike watched as yet another man claimed his wife in front of him. Under normal circumstances, this would be incredibly arousing and it still was but she could see Leila's eyes going over their partners before returning to him and he had no idea how to feel with her watching them.

The party was in full swing now, the alcohol and the dim lighting making for the perfect breeding ground for exploring. Most people around them had shed their clothes and were giving each other head whilst others were content with simply using their lips to explore as much of each other as they could without taking their clothes off.

Andre slipped the finger that had been working Sam's clit into her, causing her to let out a loud sigh. He turned her face towards him and crashed his lips against hers. His kiss was harsh and full of thinly veiled desire. Jay's kisses had been controlled but Andre's were wild, he had no intention of hiding how much he wanted Sam and it made her feel powerful, being this desired by other men.

Leila cleared her throat and Andre pulled away from Sam, his eyes darkened by desire. "Perhaps we should take this upstairs?" She proposed.

"Upstairs?" Mike asked, looking between Leila and Andre.

Andre smirked. "Of course. Or would you prefer I fuck your wife on the sofa you're sitting on?"

Mike blinked, the comment sending an instant shock of arousal through him. He turned to Leila, in an attempt to gauge how much of this she was okay with and she nodded. Andre made Sam stand before he got off the chair. He took Sam's hand and started leading her upstairs with Mike and Leila following behind them.

Sam turned around to see Mike and Leila following them. She looked at her husband and he gave her a subtle nod. They had talked about the possibility of something like this happening if they came for this party and now that it was becoming a reality, they were prepared for it. But Sam had to admit to herself that it was both thrilling and terrifying, this was only the second man she would be sleeping with since she started this whole journey and she couldn't help but wonder how she would measure up.

Her pulse quickened as they headed up the staircase. Andre turned towards her and gave her a reassuring smile which calmed her a little bit but not by much. The room he led them to was very spacious with the same soft lighting that was in the area they just left.

Andre closed the door behind them as Mike and Leila made their way into the room. He walked over to Sam and gently brushed a strand of hair behind her ear, his touch sending a thrill down her spine.

Mike sat on the armchair opposite the bed and Leila took a seat on the arm, both watching their partners intensely. Sam turned to look at them but Andre cupped her face and made her look at him.

"Forget about them. Forget that there is anyone else in this room and focus on me, only me." He leaned closer and buried his face in the crook of her neck, inhaling her scent. His hands came around her waist and grabbed her ass while he let out a soft growl.

"I can work with this." He said, squeezing her asscheeks then spanking them lightly. He brought his lips up to hers and kissed them softly, like he was testing the waters. Sam responded almost immediately, very turned on by the way Andre was taking control of the situation. He slipped his tongue into her mouth, exploring, tasting, familiarizing himself with the taste of her.

By this point, Andre was sporting a very pronounced erection. He walked Sam over to the nearby bed and pushed her into it, her breath coming out in soft gasps as Andre explored her with his hand. He grinded his erection against her, his hands moving to cup her breasts. He took his mouth away from her lips and brought them down to her chest, taking a nipple in his mouth and sucking it through her dress.

Sam threw her head back, sighing with content when she felt the wetness of his tongue as he swirled it around her nipple. She let out a gasp when he resumed sucking it with more intensity almost like a hungry child. As his mouth did its thing, one hand played with the other free nipple while the other slipped under her dress, shifting her panties to the side and penetrating her.

Andre was excited to find her already wet for him, he wanted nothing more than to skip all this preamble and bury himself inside her already but he knew he had to work her up, make her needy for him. He wanted her to beg for it before he had his way with her.

Mike could only watch as Andre fingered his wife on the bed in front of him and Leila. He was already sporting a boner and he wanted desperately to take it out of his pants and stroke it but he felt self conscious. This wasn't like the time with Jay, where it was just three of them. This time there was another pair of eyes, Leila's and he didn't know how he felt stroking himself in front of her.

But Leila wasn't the type of woman to just stand by and watch. She stood up and gingerly stepped in front of Mike, kneeling in front of him. Slowly, her hand felt up his boner and before Mike knew what was happening, she was unbuckling his pants and revealing his boner.

"What are you-" he couldn't finish his sentence because Leila's mouth quickly enveloped his dick before he could object. He let out a groan, a mix of pleasure and surprise as Leila's tongue circled and flicked against the head of his dick. She moaned as she bobbed her head up and down the shaft, earning soft gasps from Mike.

Sam heard the sounds Mike was making and turned her head, expecting to see him pleasuring himself. Instead she found Leila giving him what looked to be a very pleasurable blowjob and the red face of her husband absolutely enjoying it.

Andre took his mouth off her breast to check out what she was looking at then smirked before moving his finger faster within Sam. That brought her attention back to him as she started bucking her hips against his fingers, chasing the orgasm that was just on the horizon.

"I told you to focus on me," Andre snarled, before attacking her neck with his mouth, sucking at it hard enough to leave a mark. "Focus on how good this feels," he whispered against her neck as his finger moved faster within her. He used his thumb to circle her clit and the double stimulation was enough to send Sam over the edge.

Sam let out a long, strained moan as waves of pleasure came over her. Andre took the finger out of her then brought it up to his mouth, sucking her juices off them. She tasted sweet and Andre couldn't wait to know how she would feel when he was inside her.

Andre pushed himself off her then started unbuckling his pants, watching Sam intently as she sat up in bed, her face red and still clearly coming down from the orgasm she just experienced. "Take off your dress," he instructed, "slowly."

Sam made a show of stripping her dress of her body. She slowly raised the dress over her head, letting it drop to the floor before she unhooked her bra and took that off as well, before taking off her panties. Andre smiled as she cupped her breasts in her hands, making the look fuller.

"Fuck, I could do a lot with those. Fuck them, suck them, cum on them. There's so much I want to do to you, but for now, I need to fuck you." He said, letting his boxers drop to the floor, his huge dick standing at full attention.

He walked over to her with it in his hand, stoking it as he went along. When he stood in front of her, he traced the line of her lips with his head. "Do you see what she's doing?" He said, pointing over to Leila and Mike. Leila was holding Mike's dick in her hands and using her tongue to go up and down his shaft.

Sam nodded then looked back at Andre. "Think you can do that with this?" He pointed over to his dick that was leaking precum at this point. Sam gauged the penis in front of her face. She knew her way around a blowjob but she had never had a cock as big as Andre's in her mouth before.

"You don't have to-" Sam cut Andre off by taking his dick in her mouth, bobbing her head the way she saw Leila do earlier. "Fuck," Andre sighed, holding unto her head as his dick went in and out of Sam's mouth. The wetness and the heat of it sent shockwave after shockwave of pleasure up his body and he had to hold himself back from fucking the shit out of her mouth. Sam couldn't take the full length into her mouth but she took in what she could, tracing the head of his dick with her tongue and creating a vacuum of suction with her mouth.

She looked up at Andre and felt pride when she saw his eyes closed and his mouth open, clearly lost in the way she was sucking him. She felt the initial jealousy from watching Leila go down on Mike melt away, she could do that and even more with Andre.

Andre pushed her off him and she fell back onto the bed. He moved quickly, climbing on top of her then taking her lips harshly as he used his dick head to stroke her clit.

"I want to be inside you so bad." he groaned as he positioned himself at her entrance. He slid into her slowly, trying to get her used to the fullness of him. Sam gasped and held on to him as he buried himself fully into her.

Mike looked on as Andre thrusted into his wife, moaning as he did so. He took pride in the way Andre's mouth fell open as he moved in her, his thrusts getting more and more intense. Watching that sight and feeling the way Leila was stroking him was enough to make him burst and he came loudly, pouring cum into Leila's mouth which she happily received.

Whilst Leila cleaned up the mess that Mike had made with her mouth, Andre was driving himself into Sam forcefully. She took him eagerly, even raising her hips to meet every thrust he gave her. Andre took pleasure in the way she wrapped her legs around him, making him go deeper into her and he let out all the pent up desire he had felt earlier.

"Fuckkk," He said, leaning over and pounding into her repeatedly. She was so wet and the sound of him penetrating her was driving him over the edge. "I'm going to cum," he groaned, giving three more intense thrusts before pulling himself out of Sam and cumming all over her stomach.

"Shit," he said, chuckling as he caught his breath. "we're going to have to do this again soon."

CHAPTER ELEVEN:
Dangerous Dealings

It had been a couple of days since the very intense night at Andre and Leila's house and even though Sam and Mike discussed briefly, they both tried to avoid talking about it as much as they could. The dynamic was very new — this was the first time that Mike had been involved with someone during one of their encounters and they both didn't know what to make of it.

Sam often replayed the parts of the night where she watched Leila go down on her husband, even though it was an exciting sight she couldn't help but feel a little jealousy whenever she thought about it. Despite these feelings, she and Mike accepted an invitation from Andre and Leila to lunch at a diner central to the four of them.

The drive to the diner was quiet. Mike seemed to be preoccupied, his gaze fixed on the road but still oddly distracted. Sam opened her mouth to ask what was on his mind when his phone buzzed in the cup holder. He glanced at the screen then declined the call only for it to buzz again as the same person called again.

Sam noticed the furrow in his brow as he declined the call again and put the phone down. "Who was that?" she asked, trying to keep her tone casual even though she was a little suspicious.

"Just work stuff," Mike said with a dismissive shrug.

"Work stuff on a Saturday?" Sam asked, finding that a little suspicious. "Is everything okay?"

"It's fine, Sam. Drop it." Mike said quickly, too quickly. "There's nothing to worry about, I'll reach out to them later. Let's just focus on lunch, okay?"

Sam decided not to push further, but she couldn't help but feel a little suspicious and uneasy. She brushed off the feeling though, deciding to focus on the lunch that was supposed to be an opportunity to get to know Andre and Leila better. The last thing she wanted was to bring any tension between her and Mike into it. When they got to the diner, they found Andre and Leila already there, sitting in a booth with some drinks in front of them. Leila welcomed them with a bright smile and Andre gave Sam a lingering look before standing up to hug her and shake Mike's hand.

"We're so glad the both of you could make it." Leila said, settling into the booth beside Mike.

"We're happy we could make it. Have you guys put in an order yet?" Sam asked.

"No, not yet, we've only gotten a few drinks. We were actually waiting for you two to show up before we had anything." Andre said, handing a menu over to Sam. "Anything look good?"

Sam looked over the menu then shook her head. "I'm not really hungry, I think I'll just have a couple of iced teas." She said. Andre signaled to the waitress who took Sam's drink order. Turning to

Mike, he asked him if he was interested in anything but Mike didn't answer, seemingly engrossed by his phone.

"Mike? Man, you want anything while the waitress's here?" Andre pressed but Mike didn't answer. Leila nudged Mike and he looked up to find the entire booth looking at him and the waitress waiting patiently to take his drink order. He shook his head no, saying he wasn't interested in anything then went back to his phone.

"Mike's been dealing with some work today, I haven't even had a bit of his attention today." Sam said in a joking tone, trying to take away from the awkwardness Mike's focus on his phone was bringing.

Andre chuckled then wrapped an arm around Sam before whispering in her ear, "I guess I have to show you twice as much attention today." His statement sent goosebumps down her body. At that moment, her iced tea order came over and she eagerly downed it to calm herself down before ordering for another.

"So how long have you guys been swingers?" Sam asked, taking a sip from her iced tea then dropping it on the table.

Leila and Andre looked at each other before Leila smiled and answered. "I think the both of us have always had a healthy curiosity about things like that. We both had open relationships when we were single and this is just a natural progression of that."

"We've been in it for over five years now?" Andre asked, looking over to his wife for confirmation who then nodded. "So yeah, five years. We decided to keep our encounters with just couples because it was less messy."

Leila nodded. "The last unattached person we got involved with tried to come in between Andre and me so we both decided we don't want that type of energy in our marriage."

Sam perked up as she took a sip from her drink. "That's exactly what happened to Mike and me! Wow, what a coincidence."

"We knew you two would understand, that's why we decided to reach out. Even though we've been in this for sometime now, it's still hard to find like-minded couples." Leila said.

Sam nodded before finishing off her third glass of iced tea. "Oof, these drinks went right through me. Excuse me for a moment." She said, getting up and heading for the nearest bathroom.

She finished up and walked towards the sink, washing her hands then splashing some water on her face. She took a deep breath before turning to head back to the booth when the bathroom door creaked open. Andre slipped in, then approached her, a sly grin on his face,

"What are you doing here?" Sam whispered, her pulse quickening.

"I couldn't resist." Andre said, stepping closer to her till he was just inches away from her face. "You've been on my mind all week and I just couldn't wait."

Her breath hitched when Andre's hand found her waist and pulled her against him. "Someone might be in here." she whispered urgently.

"Then they're in for quite the show." He whispered before claiming her lips. Andre's hand wrapped around her back before slipping into her blouse and cupping her right breast. He took his mouth to her neck and kissed it, before sucking on it again.

"I really fucking want you right now," he said, breathing onto her neck. He pulled away then inspected her neck. "Looks like I left a mark last time, is it wrong that I want to leave another one?"

Sam shook her head and Andre returned his mouth to her neck, sucking at it hungrily. Her hands reached for the front of his pants and sure enough, she could feel a bulge forming. She looked around then quickly pulled him into a nearby stall.

When the both of them were safely obscured by the stall, Andre worked on taking her top off then slipped two fingers between her legs and into her. A gasp left Sam's lips causing Andre to smirk.

"You're already so wet, I love that about you." He said before tracing circles on her clit with his thumb while his two fingers moved within her. He freed a nipple from her bra and sucked on it, following Sam's senses with pleasure. She bit his shirley to cover her moans but Andre wasn't having any of that.

"I want to hear every single sound you make," he said, his fingers moving faster within her.

"But what if someone hears us?" Sam asked, still trying to keep her voice low.

"I really don't give a fuck." he said, increasing the intensity of the strokes his fingers were making inside of her. Sam threw her head back in reckless abandon and let her moans come out without any inhibition.

"Yes, that's it." Andre said, "Let it all out."

Sam buckled slightly as she came all over his fingers. He took his fingers out of her then brought them to her lips, imploring her to suck on them. "I want you to know how you taste and understand why it's so hard to resist you."

Sam sucked herself off his fingers and when she was done with that, he turned her around and bent her over, hurriedly taking his dick out and coating it with the juices between her legs.

He pushed himself into her, sighing as he did so. He presses her into the wall with each of his hard thrusts, the sound of his thighs slapping against her ass filling the air.

His hands came around and grabbed her tits while he drove himself into her. Sam could fill another orgasm building up and she backed herself up against him, begging him to go faster. Andre pounded into her faster and harder, feeling himself getting closer each time he buried himself in her.

Sam felt herself cum one more time and that seemed to be enough to drive Andre over the edge. His breath started to quicken and he moved in her faster. He leaned closer and sighed into her ear, "Fuck, this feels too fucking good."

He grunts, thrusting in one more time before pulling out of her and cumming all over the bathroom floor.

Meanwhile, back at the booth, Mike could barely focus on what Leila was saying because his phone kept buzzy and he knew that he couldn't keep ignoring it.

"That phone keeps buzzing her, you can take it, I don't mind." Leila said.

"Yeah I'm sorry, just give me a moment, I need to take this." Mike muttered, sliding out of the booth and stepping out of the diner. Now that he was alone, he could answer the call.

"You've been dodging my calls, Mike. You know the clock's ticking on this shipment, it needs to leave tonight or do I have to give this job to someone more reliable?" A gruff voice said on the other end of the phone.

Mike's jaw clenched. "We're still on for this deal. I'll get the shipment out before the day is over, just give me a bit more time."

"Fine, just get this done quickly." The gruff voice said again before ending the call.

Mike shoved his phone back into his pocket, trying to settle his anxiety over the call he just had. When he returned to the booth, he forced a smile for Leila, trying to keep himself together.

Back in the bathroom, Sam and Andre straightened themselves out and headed out, Sam first and then Andre. When they rejoined Mike and Leila back at the booth, Sam could notice a tension in Mike even though he tried to hide it. She decided not to mention it till they got home.

CHAPTER TWELVE: The Confrontation

Sam was awake in bed, staring at the ceiling as the clock ticked midnight. This was the third time this week that Mike had told her that he was working late and now he wasn't even back home. Normally she would brush it off, this wasn't the first time in their marriage that he had to stay out late for work but something about this was different. He was more guarded lately, more distant and distracted and she couldn't help but feel a little suspicious.

What could he possibly be doing? When he went out like this he was always vague. "I'm staying out late for work." he would say but what was he doing exactly? If something happened to him, what would she even tell the authorities, that she didn't know what her husband was up to at midnight?

She thought back to that night where he had hooked up with Leila. Was he cheating maybe? Sam hated that her mind went in that direction but she couldn't help it, without context her mind had to fill in the gaps however it decided it wanted to.

She knew she wasn't exactly innocent either. With Mike spending time outside so much, she had spent a lot more time with Andre than she had wanted to. He made her feel desired and wanted whereas her husband seemed to be avoiding her. She couldn't help herself but to seek Andre out.

The sound of the front door creaking open snapped her out of her late night thoughts and she sat up, listening as Mike's footsteps got closer and closer. She heard the clear sound of him fumbling with his keys, trying but failing to be quiet.

He walked into their bedroom and she flicked the lamp on, the sudden light making him squint and catching him off guard. "You're still up?" he asked, trying his best to sound casual as he took his shoes off.

"I couldn't sleep," she mumbled. "Where were you?"

"I told you before I left Sam, work stuff." You know I have to pull long hours sometimes."

"I don't know what it is you're doing that keeps you out till midnight? Do you have any idea how scary it is thinking you're out on the road in that truck, doing God knows what? What if something happened to you?"

Mike let out a frustrated sigh, this was not what he wanted to come back to after the day he had. "Look, I don't think I need to justify myself to you, not now. You know how demanding my job can be." "Oh I do, especially nowadays." She shot back. "Things are different now though, you're always distracted like the time at the diner and I can't help but wonder what's really going on."

Mike froze for a moment, not expecting his wife to call him out like that. Guilt flickered across his face for a brief moment but he quickly masked it with a dismissive shake of his head. "You're overthinking this, Sam."

"Am I?" Sam said, her voice rising. "This wouldn't have anything to do with this lifestyle would it? I know things are moving pretty fast but that doesn't mean that you have to hide things from me, I'm your wife."

Mike tightened his jaw as he looked at her. "You really want to get into this Sam? Fine, let's get into it. Let's not pretend that you haven't been getting real cozy with Andre behind my back?"

"I have no idea what you mean."

"Oh please, don't play dumb. At the diner that day, I know what you two got up to and I know you've been getting it this week when I've been out of the house. So don't come at me, talking about secrets when you've been keeping yours from me." Mike said, frustration bleeding into his voice.

"Don't make this out into a bigger deal than it is. We both agreed on Andre and Leila. You were there when we first hooked up, in fact you did the same thing with Leila."

"Yeah but the difference is, anything I did was not behind your back. You were right there when I did whatever I did with Leila but have you told me or even brought me into any of the trysts you've had with Andre recently?"

Sam kept quiet, guilt spreading on her face. "Okay I know that I haven't been completely honest but that doesn't explain the late night or all the calls you keep dodging when you're around me."

"Let it go Sam, geez. I am exhausted, I need to go to bed and you are making me so stressed out." Mike said. He knew that he couldn't keep dodging her forever but he couldn't lay it all out there for her, not now.

"Look Sam, this is business okay? And I'm handling it. So can't we just let it go and go to bed?"

"Fine," she said, her voice weary. "But don't think this is over, Mike." She turned away from Mike, pulling the covers up as she felt all the exhaustion hit her all at once. This confrontation had drained her emotionally and she didn't feel like arguing anymore. Just as she was settling into bed, her phone buzzed on her nightstand. She picked up, looking at the notification on her screen.

It was a message from Andre.

Her heart skipped a beat as she read the text: "*Thinking about you. Can we meet tomorrow? I miss our time together.*"

Before she could even process the message that came in, she felt Mike's presence behind her, his eyes narrowing as he leaned over to see the screen.

"Seriously, Sam?" His voice was cold, the frustration from earlier creeping back in. "You're seriously planning another meetup right in front of me?"

Sam tensed, already knowing where this was headed. "It's not like that! I haven't even responded. "

"Oh but you were going to, what were you going to do? Sneak off to see him while I'm busting my ass off out there? " Mike scoffed, crossing his arms.

"Oh c'mon. You just said you were exhausted and now you're bringing up another argument out of nowhere? " Sam shot back,

"Don't play the victim here!" Mike's voice rose, his anger clear. "We agreed that if we're going to do this, it would be with communication and transparency. But you're keeping secrets now, seeing Andre without telling me. That was never part of the deal, Sam."

"Maybe I wouldn't be doing it if you weren't so focused on whatever shady business you're mixed up in," Sam snapped. "Disappearing late at night, taking calls you won't explain? You're shutting me out, Mike, so can you really blame me for looking for a way to keep busy? —

"You're not the only one with issues, Sam." Mike said, his expression now shifting to one of hurt. "I've been dealing with the fact that you're getting closer to Andre, more than we agreed to. I see how you look at him, how you're letting this become more than just sex.

And what about me, Sam? I don't mind what you do with him but why are you hiding it from me?"

Sam felt her defenses falter, guilt gnawing at her. "Yeah well, now you know how I felt watching Leila feel you up that night." She said, in an effort to mask her guilt.

"That was different and you know it. You were there, you didn't say anything afterward, I thought you were okay with it."

"Well I wasn't. It was hot yeah but it wasn't part of the deal either, I was blindsided and the most annoying part is, we never even talked about it afterward."

Mike's jaw tightened, his voice low. "So what do we do now, Sam? The whole point of doing this was so things wouldn't get messy but it looks like it's too late for that."

"I don't know. But I do know that this isn't what I wanted. I thought exploring this would bring us closer, that it would be something we could share together. But now...I don't want to fight about this anymore."

Mike sighed. "You're right. I don't want to fight either. We stopped being honest with each other, and now we're both doing things we said we wouldn't."

A heavy silence hung between them as they both struggled to find the right words. Finally, Sam took a deep breath, her voice softer now. "Maybe we need to stop seeing Andre and Leila. It's clear this isn't working for either of us. We've lost sight of what really matters—us."

Mike nodded slowly, though the decision felt bittersweet. "Yeah. This was supposed to be the solution to our problem but now it feels like it's coming between us, just like Jay tried to." ,

"Maybe we need to take a step back and figure out how to come back at this?"

"I think that's a good idea. So that's it, no more Andre and Leila?"

Sam nodded, although she felt that was a decision that was hard to make. She would miss Andre but nothing was worth losing the trust her husband had in her.

CHAPTER THIRTEEN: The Proposal

Mike stopped doing late-night deliveries for a couple of days. Anytime the dealer called him, he would make up an excuse on why he couldn't go. He did this to prevent any more fights between him and Sam. They had promised to be more honest so this was his way of doing that. Things seemed to be going okay, that is until they got an invitation from Andre and Leila.

They hadn't heard from them since Sam ignored the text Andre sent. Now he reached out again, sending an invitation to another swinger's party, with the promise of new faces and opportunities to meet others in the lifestyle.

"What do you think about this?" Sam asked Mike, showing him the message that evening while they were having dinner. "I know what we said," she began carefully, watching his reaction. "But don't you think this would be a good opportunity?"

"A good opportunity to do what?" Mike asked, chewing his food a little bit too loudly.

"To meet other people. We don't have to get involved with Andre and Leila but that doesn't mean we have to give up this lifestyle, you like it right?"

Mike thought about it and she was right, he did enjoy these sexcapades of theirs and he had to admit that it felt a little hard giving all of that up so easily. "You're right, I do like it,"

"So what do you say? We can go as a couple and just have fun then see what's out there."

"So we go to the party for us, not for them?"

"Exactly." Sam nodded. "No strings, no pressure. We can keep to ourselves if we want. We've talked about how we might be interested in exploring this lifestyle with other people, right? This could be a good way to dip our toes in without getting too deep too fast."

Mike was quiet for a moment, his gaze fixed on the invite on Sam's phone. Part of him was wary, it hadn't been long since they'd agreed to distance themselves from Andre and Leila, and going back into that environment felt like a risk. But on the other hand, he didn't want to retreat into the comfort of the routine their sex life had become prior to these new adventures Sam got involved in.

"I'm in but no secrets this time okay?"

"Deal." Sam's smile widened, relieved that they were on the same page. "This could be fun, you know? We're finally figuring out how to do this in a way that works for us."

"So when's the party?" Mike asked, going back to his food.

"It's tomorrow. Gosh, I wonder what I'm going to wear."

"Just wear any old dress, you'll look gorgeous." Mike responded.

The next day came by pretty quickly and soon Mike and Sam were on their way to the party. The party was already in full swing by the time they showed up. It was pretty similar to the first one, taking place in Andre and Leila's big suburban house, filled to the brim with people that were dressed to impress.

But this time, the action started earlier than expected. As they made their way through the main room, they couldn't help but notice couples already indulging openly in one another, the air thick with the scent of sex and alcohol.

Sam tried to ignore the growing heat in her body as they passed groups lounging on velvet couches, hands and lips exploring freely. Mike walked beside her, his hand resting possessively on the small of her back. They passed by a couple who were having sex on a nearby couch and headed deeper into the house, in search of Andre and Leila.

The sound of laughter drew their attention toward the bar where they spotted Andre and Leila, effortlessly mingling with the other guests. Sam's heart skipped a beat when she laid eyes on Andre. She hadn't been sure what it would feel like seeing them again but there was no doubt about it, this couple was still as charismatic as ever.

As if sensing their presence, Andre turned and locked eyes with them, his smile widening. He nudged Leila, and the couple made their way over, greeting Sam and Mike with warmth.

"I'm so glad you two could make it," Andre said, his deep voice smooth as ever. He leaned in to kiss Sam's cheek, lingering just a moment longer than polite. Leila greeted Mike the same way, a knowing glint in her eyes as she pulled back.

"We wouldn't miss it," Sam replied, trying to keep her voice steady despite the nerves tingling under her skin. Mike nodded, gripping his wife's hand a little tighter.

Leila waved over a server holding a tray of colorful cocktails. "You have to try these, they're a house specialty," she said, handing them each a glass. "They'll help you loosen up."

Sam eyed the drink cautiously before taking a sip. It was strong, much stronger than she expected, but the flavors masked the potency. Mike took a long swallow and raised his eyebrows in surprise. "They weren't kidding," he muttered under his breath, making Sam chuckle.

With drinks in hand, Leila and Andre led them to a waiter corner where the music wasn't loud. They exchanged some small talk, sipping the drinks in their hands. Sam could feel herself getting more comfortable and she eyed the couples she could see in the soft lighting, wondering which one of them would make a good new conquest.

Andre noticed her wandering eyes and then cleared his throat. "Listen guys, we have to confess that we had an ulterior motive inviting you out here tonight."

"Oh?" Sam said, the buzz from the cocktails making her mind fuzzy.

Andre looked at his wife and she nodded. "We've been thinking," he said, his gaze shifting between Sam and Mike. "We had such a good time together, and we think there's more potential here... something a bit more long-term, if you're open to it."

Leila chimed in, her voice excited. "We're talking about something exclusive, a regular arrangement between just the four of us. No need to search for new partners every time. We're all comfortable with each other, so why not take this to the next level? Andre likes being with you Sam and I like being with Mike so we could make this a regular partner swap till whenever we decide to end it."

Sam wasn't sure how she felt about this, she looked over at Mike but it was like his mind wasn't even here. He was unusually quiet and he had been glancing at his phone more than once, fidgeting like he was anxious.

Andre took Sam to a corner and leaned closer to her "So, what do you think?" he asked smoothly, "A long-term arrangement between just us four makes sense, doesn't it? We've already established trust, and it's clear we have chemistry."

Sam bit her lip. She was about to respond when she noticed movement out of the corner of her eye. Mike was excusing himself from Leila, his expression tight as he muttered something and walked away with his phone clutched in his hand.

"I'll be right back," Sam said to Andre, forcing a smile as she moved to follow Mike. Andre's eyes followed her, wondering what this was about.

Sam trailed Mike down a dim hallway that led away from the main area of the party. She could hear his voice as she approached, the tension in his tone unmistakable.

"I said I'm handling it," Mike hissed into the phone, his back turned to her. "I don't need you threatening me, I'll have the shipment moved tonight. Just back off, or we're done." His voice dropped lower, but the edge in it was clear. "You think sending me those texts was smart? I don't care who you are; you push me, and I'll push back harder."

Sam's heart lurched at his words. Shipment? Threats? Her mind raced with questions, trying to piece together what she was overhearing.

She stepped closer, her pulse pounding. "Mike, what the hell is going on?" she demanded.

Mike spun around, startled. For a split second, guilt flashed across his face before it hardened into a defensive expression. "It's nothing, Sam," he said quickly, slipping his phone into his pocket. "Just work stuff. You wouldn't understand."

"Work stuff, again?" Sam scoffed, crossing her arms. "You're talking about shipments at a party? You've been acting weird all night, what is going on?"

Mike's eyes darted around as if searching for the right words. He opened his mouth to speak, but Sam cut him off, her voice rising. "What are you really involved in, Mike? What have you been hiding?"

Before he could answer, the sound of approaching footsteps interrupted them. Andre appeared, a concerned look on his face. "Everything okay here?" he asked, glancing between them with a raised eyebrow.

Sam shot Andre a sharp look. "Not really. But I'm handling it, please give me a second."

Andre nodded and walked away, leaving Sam and Mike alone.

Mike's jaw clenched, the tension in his body palpable. He was cornered, and he knew it.

"Well Mike? I'm waiting, what's the excuse this time?"

What was Mike hiding exactly?

THE END BOOK 2

CHAPTER FOURTEEN: The Unveiling

Sam and Mike faced each other on the front porch outside Andre's house, the bass from the music inside loud as the thumping in Mike's chest. Andre's proposal still hung in the air but that was the last thing on any of their minds. Mike was clearly nervous, his hand shaking despite the phone he held in it. Sam on the other hand, her patience was wearing thin and she was getting tired of waiting for an answer to the simple question she asked.

"I won't ask you again Mike, who was that on the phone? And I swear to God if you tell me it was work, I will end you." She demanded, the frustration evident in her voice.

Mike tried to think of the right thing to say, his mind was racing as he tried to come up with a plausible excuse for what he was doing. He had no idea how much she had heard but he knew that it was enough to incriminate him in her mind.

Sam looked into his eyes, looking for any hint of sincerity in them but she didn't find any. Instead, she could feel his hesitation and the silence between stretched until it became too uncomfortable to ignore.

Fed up with his silence, Sam threw her hands up, sighing loudly. "Fine, if you won't tell me then I'm done." She turned on her heel and headed towards the car.

"Wait, Sam where are you going?" Mike called out to her.

"Anywhere you're not!" Sam shouted at him, getting into the car and starting it. Mike panicked and raced towards the car, grabbing the keys out of the ignition.

"Give me back those keys, Mike. I don't want to be here anymore." Sam said, reaching out for the keys in Mike's hands.

"Please Sam, at least let me drive. I don't want you out on the streets in this state please." His tone was soft and the concern in it made Sam calm down. Rolling her eyes, she got out of the driver's seat and went round the car to the passenger side.

The ride home was uncomfortable to say the least, Sam looked out the window wondering just how deep Mike's deceit went. Mike could only grip the steering wheel as hard as he could, knowing that he would have no choice but to come clean otherwise Sam might do something drastic.

When they finally got home, Sam wasted no time. As soon as they were behind closed doors, she turned on her husband and demanded his attention once again. Her voice was shaky but it came out firm as she made her frustrations clear.

"Mike, I need the truth. Now. No more lies, no more half-truths, no dismissing this. What is going on with you? Please be honest with me." Sam paused as she considered another possibility. "Are you...are you sleeping with someone else?"

"What?! Oh my goodness, no. No! I'm not sleeping with anyone. It's nothing like that I promise you." Mike said, quick to reassure her.

"If it's not cheating then what the hell is going on here Mike? You've been so shady for a long time now, you're fielding calls whenever you're around me, you're taking secret calls. C'mon you have to admit that all of that looks a little suspicious."

Mike sighed, knowing his wife was right. "You're right, I understand how it looks suspicious, really I do. But the thing is, it's hard to be honest with you right now."

"Hard? What's hard about it? You were the one that made a big deal about us being honest with each other, so why are you taking your word back now?" Sam started to say, "What is so hard that you can't just tell me?"

"I'm involved in things Sam, things that you wouldn't understand. Things that could put you and I in danger, I can't just come out and tell you these things because it would seriously be putting you in danger."

"What is this? A gangster movie? You are a middle aged man Mike, in your forties. What could you possibly be involved in that is so hard to just come out and say? Honestly I don't know what to think here, I'm really disappointed. I thought I could trust you."

Mike exhaled deeply, Sam's words cutting deep into him. He didn't want to lose her trust, not over this. He hated to think that he had disappointed her in some way because of what he was doing but what was the guarantee that she wouldn't be disappointed if he told her what was happening.

The weight of his secret was heavy in his chest and he wanted nothing more than to be honest. He knew he had no choice but to come clean so he looked into his wife's eyes and began to speak.

"Sam, I never wanted you to know about this. In fact I never wanted you to ever find out like this." He paused and took another deep breath to steady himself. "I'm involved in something, something dangerous. It's something I don't want to drag you into, which is why I have kept it hidden from you all this time."
Sam's heart sank, what was he talking about? What has her husband gotten himself into? "W-what is it Mike, tell me. I'm sure we can figure it out together. Is it about your job?"

"It's not just a job...It has to do with something illegal..." Mike paused, unable to come clean fully.

"For goodness sake, Mike. Just spit it out already!" Sam shouted.

"Drugs okay? It's drugs, I'm dealing drugs. I make deliveries, running packages to discrete locations on behalf of this dealer."

Sam's breath catches in her throat and she tries to process everything her husband just said to her. "You're involved in...drugs?" she whispered, disbelief flashing across her face.

Mike nods, unable to meet her gaze. Sam took a moment to process what he just said to her "Mike, how could you get involved in something like this? Did you even think about what you were getting yourself into? Do you have any idea how dangerous that would be?"

"Look, I know that you have a lot of questions right now..." Mike started.

"I do have a lot of questions! Starting with 'what the hell were you thinking?!' How long has this been going on? Why would you get yourself into something like this? What if something had happened to you?" Sam said, throwing different questions at him.

Mike ran his hand over his face and walked over to a nearby chair to take a seat. He could barely stand, he was terrified. This was exactly what he wanted to avoid, he hadn't wanted her to know what was happening.

"Everything started over a year ago. Things were hard at the warehouse, I wasn't making enough trips and then this came along somehow. I only wanted to do it for a couple of months, make a little extra money on the side but then it got out of control. Before I knew it, I was way too deep and I couldn't leave."

"Is that what all those calls you've been ignoring are about? They are deliveries you're supposed to make on behalf of this drug boss?"

"Yes but not in the way you think. I stopped going out on their behalf and now I'm getting threats. That was what the call tonight was about, I think I'm in too deep and I don't know what to do."

"I can't believe this. You've been doing this for over a year? I've been by myself for months, waiting for you. Sometimes I spent the night all on my own and all that time you were dealing drugs like some...criminal?" Sam could feel her head spinning and she stumbled back till she bumped into a chair. Shaking, she took a seat as everything started to sink in. Her husband was a drug dealer, a 45 year old drug dealer.

"You have to quit, Mike." Sam said, her voice coming out much steady. "There's no future in that sort of thing, there's too much risk."

"It's not that easy, Sam. I just ignored a couple calls but look at the way I'm getting treated. Imagine what could happen if I left. They could hunt me down and do unspeakable things to me...I don't want that."

"So what do you want? You want to keep pushing drugs till you die? Look at you, you're not built like a criminal. I know it's hard but we have to figure out a way to get you out of this, you have to promise me you will try to leave this behind."

Mike nodded. "I promise Sam but I'm going to be honest, I'm scared."

"I know you are but you aren't alone anymore. I'm sure if we put our heads together, we can figure something out. I'm here for you now, everything will be okay."

CHAPTER FIFTEEN: A Dangerous Proposition

It had been a couple of days since Mike revealed that he was into the drug trade to his wife, Sam, and since then he was able to catch his breath. For a moment, it looked like things were finally getting calmer, that was until he got a call from none other than Tyrell.

Of course this wasn't the first time that Tyrell has reached out to Mike, but in Mike's experience he only got contacted by the head of the drug trade whenever things weren't going well. If he had to get a message to Mike, he usually did it using goons at his disposal. So for Tyrell to be calling him now, it meant that he was in serious trouble.

Mike's blood ran cold as he saw the name on the screen. Mike had been getting calls from some of Tyrell's men non-stop over the past few days, each time with more persistence. Mike had been avoiding those calls, hoping that he could buy some time to figure out how to get out of this mess but now it looked like he was out of time and he would have no choice but to face the music.

Tyrell wasn't a man to be kept waiting.

Reluctantly, Mike picked up the phone, his heart pounding in his chest. "Hello?"

"Don't fucking 'hello' me," Tyrell's voice came from the other end of the call, clearly irritated. "My men have been trying to reach you for days now and you've been icing them out. I don't like to get involved in petty shit like this so I'm going to give you the opportunity to explain yourself.

"Look, boss..."

"Ah ah, don't waste my time man. Get right to the point, why the fuck have you been ghosting?"

Mike squeezed his eyes shut as if that would protect him from Tyrell. "Look man, I've just been dealing with a couple things and I only wanted to take a few days..."

"A few days??? It's been weeks since you've been out on the road. And for what? You're dodging calls and you aren't making me any money, if you're not making me any money then you're dead to me." Tyrell's voice echoed through the phone, it was cold.

"It's just not a good time..." Mike started to say.

"I don't give a fuck about your time. You think I care what kind of time you're having? The only thing I care about is that you handle your business and make me money. Because of you, profits are low and you know how I feel about dwindling profits."

"I know..."

"So get back out there and do what you're supposed to do!" Tyrell shouted through the phone.

"But I can't." Mike croaked out.

"Why the fuck not?" Tyrell asked.

"That's what I need to talk to you about in person, I don't know if that would be possible at all."

There was a pause on the other end of the phone that put Mike on edge. Eventually Tyrell's voice came through the phone. "You better not be playing games with me Mike."

"No, no games," Mike said quickly. He got the sense that he was wearing Tyrell's patience thin. "Just let me say my piece and then I'll get out of your hair."

Tyrell went silent for a moment, then he finally said, "Fine, but if you're wasting my time then you're going to regret it."

"Thank you so much, where can I meet you?" Mike asked.

"I'll text you the details, now lose this number." That was the last thing Mike heard Tyrell say before he hung up. All he could do was look at the phone in his hand, his mind racing. He got the feeling that the conversation would be difficult, especially since Tyrell was the kind of man who didn't take too kindly to betrayal. But he had made Sam a promise and he was determined to keep it so he could earn her trust back.

Sam walked into the room, looking concerned. "I couldn't help but overhear your conversation. Who was that?" She asked, her voice soft.

"It was Tyrell, the leader of the drug trade. He doesn't call often but he's pretty pissed that I'm not out there making deliveries."

"So what did you guys talk about?"

"Nothing, I just asked for an meeting with him and I'm going to meet up with him soon."

Sam knew what that meant. Mike was going to plead his case in front of the boss himself. She knew that there was very little possibility Mike could get out of it, but she also knew that any more involvement in that life would lead to nothing but his downfall.

"Mike..." Sam started to say.

Mike nodded, almost like he knew what she wanted to say. "I'll be safe, don't worry about it."

It took a while but Tyrell texted Mike the details of their meetings like he said he would. Mike was to meet him at the nearest warehouse where they stored goods the next day, around noon.

Tyrell was waiting for Mike at the warehouse. As he made his way to the rendezvous point, all Mike could feel was nervousness. He had no idea what waited for him once he crossed the threshold into the warehouse. For all he knew, Tyrell could get rid of him as soon as he laid eyes on him.

The warehouse was quiet, there was no one in there and nothing apart from some stacks of wooden crates and metal containers that lined the walls. Tyrell emerged from the corner, then leaned against a stack of crates, his arms crossed across his chest and his eyes focused on Mike entirely.

Tyrell was younger than Mike, being only 39 but he carried himself with a confidence that made him appear much older. His skin was a deep, rich shade of brown and his head was completely shaved clean while he sported a goatee and mustache combos. He was wearing a black leather jacket underneath which was a plain white shirt. He looked alert like he was ready to stroke at any moment.

He was intimidating and that did nothing to help Mike's nervousness.

Mike stopped walking a few feet away from Tyrell. He couldn't read the expression on his face and that made it hard to tell what kind of mood he was in. "Thank you for meeting me, you look impressive as always." He said, trying to keep his voice steady.

Tyrell smirked and looked Mike up and down, "You look like shit, Mike," He said, ending his statement with a chuckle.

Mike didn't know how to respond, he waited until Tyrell finished laughing at his expense and then spoke up. "I'm sure you're wondering why I asked to meet you in person."

"I have to admit, I am curious but again, I don't like people wasting my time so get to the point Mike."

Okay, Mike thought, he wasn't in the mood for small talk. "I'm here to tell you that I want out."

The smirk on Tyrell's face vanished and it was replaced by a cold, annoyed look. "Out?" he repeated. "What do you mean, you want out?"

"I mean I'm done Mr. Tyrell." Mike said as firmly as he could. "I don't want to do this anymore. No more deals, no more deliveries, I have a family and I want that to be my focus right now."

Tyrell didn't say anything, the silence between them stretched for what felt like forever until he suddenly burst into laughter. "*I have a family and I want to focus on that,*" Tyrell mocked, "Man, you ain't the only one who's got a family. We all got families but we get our shit done and keep them out of it. So why are you coming to me with this weak ass excuse?"

Mike swallowed, "I just don't want to do this anymore, man. I've done so much for you already, I'm a middle aged man, I'm not about that life."

"Don't piss me off." Tyrell warned. "You think this is something that you can just walk away from? You're in deep, You fucking owe me and I don't let debts go that easily."

"Whatever it is I owe, I'll pay it-"

"With what money? You're in this business because you're broke as fuck." Tyrell said.

"What are you not getting? I'm done with the drugs." Mike said, standing his ground. His voice was firm, the most it had been since he walked in. But would it be enough to convince Tyrell to let him go?

Tyrell looked at him for a long time with his jaw clenched. He took in Mike's demeanor and he had to admit that he admired him for standing his ground.

"Let me make something clear to you, Mike. You cannot leave and you cannot buy your way out of this. If you think that then you're dumber than I thought you were. But I'm going to cut you a deal."

"Oh?"

"Yeah, I'll give you some time to think about it. Get your mind right, if you still insist on this 'I wanna leave' bs then I'll have no choice but to take drastic actions."

"How drastic?" Mike asked, swallowing.

"Let's hope you never find out." Tyrell said, turning away from Mike and walking back into the shadows.

Mike's heart started to race as he realized how bad the situation was. He couldn't believe how naïve he was, thinking he had a choice in this. Tyrell would never let him go that easily.

CHAPTER SIXTEEN:
Uninvited Guests

Sam was all by herself in the apartment, Mike had gone grocery shopping. Ever since he got back from Tyrell's, they had been laying low and keeping to themselves but they had no choice but to let Mike go out there and shop for food. Sam had never been this anxious before, her mind kept racing with possibilities. Her husband was basically a drug dealer and now he had gotten them into a terrible situation.

She was still pacing when she heard a loud, aggressive knock echo through the living room, causing her to jump. She had no idea who was at the door and why they would be hitting it so hard. She wasn't even expecting anybody.

Her heart pounded as she walked towards the door, the sound of her footsteps loud on the hardwood floor. The knock came again, more insistent this time. She hesitated as she reached for the doorknob, her hand trembling. She didn't know what was on the other side of that door but she had the feeling it couldn't be good.

Just as she was about to turn the door knob, the door burst open and three tall, hooded men trooped in. They were all big, muscular and dressed in dark clothes. The one in front, the biggest out of the three, had a hard look in his eyes.

"Where's Mike?" the biggest out of the three men demanded, his voice was low and menacing.

Sam swallowed. She knew instinctively that these were Tyrell's men, who else could they be?

"Where the fuck is Mike?!" The man demanded again, this time pointing a gun directly at Sam's head.

"I-I don't know," Sam stammered, trying not to show her fear at the gun pointed at her. "He's not here, he's not here right now."

"Bullshit," The guy said, turning to the other two men with him. "Search the place, he's got to be hiding somewhere."
The other two men nodded and went into the house to search for Mike, leaving Sam alone to who was no doubt the leader.

"Now, let me tell you something." The leader said, stepping closer, his presence intimidating. "If my men find your husband somewhere in this house, I'm gonna blow your brains out."

Sam shook her head, her voice trembling. "I swear, he's not here. I don't know where he is, he never tells me where he's going."

The leader's eyes narrowed as he studied her, he was clearly unconvinced. He yelled out to the other men, wanting to know their progress.

"Y'all find anything?!" he called out.

"Not yet boss!" One of them called out to him.

Sam could hear the sound of them breaking into rooms and ransacking them. She didn't know what to do, how to call them off or get them to leave. If they didn't find Mike, what were they going to do with her?"

The other two men came out from the inner rooms of the house and made their way to their leader.

"He's not here boss." One of them asked.

The leader cursed under his breath. "Do you think he knew we were coming?" He asked

"Nah, I doubt it. But what are we going to do?" Another masked man asked.

"We can't go back to boss man Tyrell empty handed, he's still waiting on his answer and he don't like to wait. So we have to wait till Mike comes around and jump his ass." The leader said, rationalizing their next plan of action.

Sam couldn't let that happen. She had to keep them away from Mike somehow. She looked directly at the leader, her mind racing with ideas on how to get them to leave the house before Mike gets back.

"Please," she begged, her voice a whisper, "Please don't hurt my husband. You can pretend like you never got here, I'll do anything." The leader smirked, amused by her fear. He stepped closer, till his face was too close to hers. Sam could feel the heat radiating off him, the heady mix of sweat and cologne making its way to her nose. He reached it and tucked a loose strand of hair behind her ear.

"Anything?" he asked, dropping his voice to a whisper.

Sam nodded. She knew she was making a dangerous deal but she had no idea how else to get out of this situation. If she could do something to please these men and make them leave her husband alone she would do it. She didn't have much of a choice.

The leader's smirk turned into a cruel smile. "Good," he started to say, "then suck my dick."

Sam's eyes widened in shock at this proposal. She couldn't believe that he could be so bold as to suggest something like that.

"I can't do that." She protested.

"Bitch, you're the one that said anything." He said, standing up and unbuckling his pants. Sam and the other two men watched as he pulled out his cock, long and thick then stroked it to make it hard.

Sam looked over the penis that was in front of her. It was big, bigger than Jay's and Andre's and those two had pretty big ones too. If she had to guess, it would be around 9/10 inches. Just like him, it was intimidating as well.

"So what's it going to be?" The leader asked, still stroking his dick.

Sam watched as it got progressively harder. She swallowed, feeling a bit of arousal and anxiety about possibly putting that in her mouth. "I can't suck on that."

"Well you better fucking try, otherwise your husband's going to be on the other end of this," he nodded his head towards the gun in left hand.

Sam took a deep breath then crawled over to him, kneeling in front of his penis. She took it in her hands and it felt a little heavy. Sam took a deep breath before wetting her tongue, sticking out then trailing it all over the head.

"Oh, okay..." The leader sighed, holding on to Sam's head as she used her tongue to go up and down the shaft of his penis, wetting it thoroughly. She cupped her mouth around the head of the sick, swirling her tongue in circles around it whilst making a suction with her cheeks.

She wasn't ready to take it all in yet but there was a lot she could do before trying to shove it down her throat. She took her mouth of it, spat in her hand and then started stroking him, slowly, making twisting motions as her hand went up and down the shaft.

"Now that's what I'm talking about," The leader said, leaning his hips forward to be closer to Sam. She brought her mouth back to his dickhead, making swirling motion with her tongue while her hand went up and down his shaft.

The other two men are visibly aroused at this point and their erections we're straining against their pants. They wished in that moment that they had been the ones to take Sam up on her offer, the urge to cum in her pretty pink mouth was strong.

Sam worked the leader's penis until she felt she was comfortable taking a reasonable portion of it into her mouth. She trailed her tongue up and down his dick, wetting it to her satisfaction until finally she put her mouth to the dickhead and sucked it into her mouth, earning a long groan from the man in front of her.

"Yeah, that's right. Take this dick." He said, grabbing Sam's head with two of his hands and shoving his dick in and out of her mouth. Sam was taken aback by the sudden brute force from this man and tried her best not to gag as his dick went deeper and deeper into her mouth.

The man bobbed Sam's head up and down his dick, going deeper every time until he was hitting the back of her throat. He slowly pulled out of her mouth, his dick glistening with her saliva and smirked.

"Nah, I gotta tap that." He said, looking down at Sam. "Take off those pajamas."
"No," Sam said, shaking her head. She held her clothes closer to her body, as if to hide from his gaze.

"The fuck you mean no?" The leader said, his eyes narrowing in anger.

"The deal was I suck your dick and you leave my husband alone. If you're going to fuck then I'm going to need more from you." Sam said, trying not to let her fear show. She was taking a huge gamble, after all this man could just force her into doing what he wanted but she was going to take this chance.

"What more do you need?" He asked.

"Tell me how to contact Tyrell and you can do whatever you want to me." Sam said, her voice firm.

The other men burst into laughter but the leader stayed calm. He held his dick in his hands, stroking it as he was deep in thought. Eventually he smirked then said.

"You've got yourself a deal."

CHAPTER SEVENTEEN: The Indecent Proposal

Sam was elated that this man took up her offer. She took off her pajama top, slowly revealing the red lacy bra that was underneath. Carefully, she undid the clasps of her bra and let it fall to the ground.

"Damn, those tits are huge." The leader exclaimed, his eyes focused on Sam's heaving bosom. Sam slowly took off the rest of her pajamas until she was completely naked in front of the man. She crawled on all fours towards him, taking his dick into her mouth once again. She bobbed her head up and down the length that she could take in, creating suction by sucking her cheeks in.

The leader pushed her off him and she fell on her back onto the floor. He moved quickly, climbing on top of her and rubbing his dick against her vulva.

"Damn, I didn't think you'd be this wet. You a freak huh?" He said, before burying himself into her. "Oh shit." He said as he pushed himself deeper into her until he was completely up to the hilt in her.

"This bitch took all of that." One of the other men said in shock. He turned to his colleague to find that he had his dick out and was stroking it rapidly, his eyes completely on Sam and their leader.

The leader was different from Jay and Andre. Those men had been gentle, and tried to please her as best that they could. This man on the other hand, his strokes were as hard and rough as he was. He was not gentle by any means, pinning Sam down with his full weight, locking his arms around her and thrusting with a force that could only come from a virile young man.

It was uncomfortable for Sam but it was strangely arousing, especially when he grabbed unto her breasts and squeezed, swearing as he did so. Before she knew what was happening, the other two men came around. One of them knelt with his dick in his hand, shoving it into her mouth whilst the other one stood and watched the scene in front of him.

Sam had a full view of this other man's balls as he shoved his dick in and out of her mouth whilst their leader shoved himself in and out of her. "Holy shit," she heard the leader say, "this bitch bouta make me cum." he groaned.

He gave six more hard thrusts, moaning as he did so then pulled out of Sam rapidly and came all over her stomach. He groaned as rope after rope of cum shot out of his penis unto her skin. The other two men followed, the one with the balls in her face came full on in her mouth whilst the other one shot ropes of cum all over her boobs.

The three men stood up and started cleaning themselves up, leaving Sam in a mix of her juices and theirs. She stood up and watched them tuck their dicks back into their pants then putting their clothes back on.

"It's time for you to hold up your end of the bargain." Sam said, trying to put on a brave front.

"Oh yeah? And what bargain was that again?" The leader asked as he fastened his belt.

Sam's blood ran cold. Had she just given up her body for no reason? Had this man literally screwed her over?

"You're supposed to leave my husband alone and tell me how I can contact Tyrell." Sam said, raising her voice.

The three men looked at each other and smirked. The leader took a flip phone out of his jeans and threw it over at Sam who was still covered in cum. She caught the phone and looked it over, then looked up at the leader curiously.

"Call up boss man Tyrell on it. I can't say he'll be happy to hear from you but knock yourself out." The leader said as he and the men made their way towards the door that they had knocked down earlier.

"And what about my husband?" Sam called out to them.

"We'll leave him alone for now but Tyrell isn't done with him yet that's for sure." He said before leaving.
Sam lay on the living room floor, her body trembling with both exhaustion and shame. She didn't move for a long time, just started at the ceiling as she tried to process everything that just happened. She could still feel the roughness from the encounter, the way they had used her without a second thought. She didn't have time to dwell on what she experienced though, all she could was pick herself up. After all, she had done it for her husband.

She got up and made her way to the bathroom, placing the flip phone on a coffee table nearby. She needed to clean herself, maybe it would help her forget everything that just happened. She stepped into the shower and turned on the water, it was scalding hot but she didn't care.

She scrubbed her skin, until it was raw, as if that would scrub away everything that happened. She turned the water off and stepped out, wrapping herself in a towel. She went into the bedroom to dry off and thought about what she was going to say to Mike when he got back, how she would explain all of this to him.

She started drying her hair when she heard the front door creak. Her heater jumped into her throat as she quickly pulled on a bathrobe. Had those men come back, did they want to go back on the deal they made? Had they changed their minds so soon? Her mind raced as she stood by the bedroom door, waiting for any indication on who was at the front door.

"Sam?" Mike's voice echoed throughout the apartment. She could hear the panic and worry in his voice. She breathed a sigh of relief and walked out to meet him.

"Sam! Oh my goodness, are you okay? I saw the broken door, what happened? Is everything alright?" Mike said, dropping down everything in his hands and stretching his arms out to embrace his wife. She fell into his arms, squeezing her eyes so tears wouldn't fall. "Look at you, you're shaking. What happened?"

Mike looked down at her, his gaze soft. He was worried, he had no idea what happened here and he just hoped that Sam was okay.

Sam forced a smile but he could see that it didn't reach her eyes. "I'm fine, Mike. I'm okay, really."

Mike frowned, he was not convinced. "Sam, talk to me, clearly something happened here."

Sam looked away, unable to meet his gaze. "It was Tyrell's men," she admitted. "They came looking for you. They burst in and started demanding to know where you were. I was so confused, I didn't know what to do."

Mike's face paled and he clenched his hands into fists. "What did they do? Did they hurt you? I swear if they hurt you, I'll kill Tyrell with these hands."

Sam swallowed hard. She knew she couldn't lie to him. He deserved to know the truth. "They didn't hurt me, Mike," she said, her voice trembling. "But they were going to hurt you or even worse... unless I did something for them."

Mike's expression darkened, his eyes narrowing in anger. "What did they make you do?"

"I didn't want to do it but it was either that or let them do something to me and you. I told them I would do anything to keep you safe and then they made me..."

"Made you what, Sam?" Mike asked, his jaw clenched.

Sam forced herself to speak. "They made me sleep with them," she confessed, her voice cracking. "It was the only way to make them leave you alone. They left me this," she added, gesturing toward the flip phone on the table. "They said I could use it to reach Tyrell."

Mike staggered back, the color draining from his face as her words sank in. For a moment, he was too stunned to speak, his mind struggling to comprehend what she had done. When he finally found his voice, it came out hoarse and thick with emotion. "Sam... you didn't have to..."

"I had no choice," Sam interrupted, her voice coming out firm. "They were going to hurt you, Mike. I couldn't let that happen. What would you have me do?!"

Mike's anger faded, replaced by a deep sadness. He pulled Sam into his arms, holding her tightly. He didn't know what to say, didn't know how to make it better. After all this was his mess, he had brought this to their door. He had failed to protect her and that's why she did what she did.

He could only be grateful that his wife was willing to go so far for him.

He walked them over to their bedroom and Sam sat on the edge of their bed, her hand clenched in her laps. Mike stood across from her guilt weighing on him. Sam looked up at her husband and said, very firmly:

"I'm going to meet up with Tyrell."

CHAPTER EIGHTEEN: A Dangerous Choice

Mike snapped his head up, his eyes wide with shock, "What? No way Sam, Absolutely not. You're not going anywhere near that man."

Sam shook her head. "I have to, Mike. We can't keep living like this, with these men hanging over our heads. I need to do something to get us out of this mess."

"I already tried and that didn't work, what makes you think you can make any difference?" Mike asked, frustration seeping in.

"I at least have to try! It's not like things could get worse for us, we are currently living under the tyranny of a drug lord!"

Mike moved closer, his hands resting on her shoulders as he looked down at her with pleading eyes. "Sam, please. You've already done more than enough. You shouldn't have to suffer again because of my mistakes. I should be the one to deal with this."

Sam reached up, placing her hand over his. "I've already suffered, Mike," she said quietly. "But this isn't just about what I've been through. I can't live with that fear hanging over us."

Mike's grip tightened on her shoulders. "And you think going to Tyrell will solve anything? He's dangerous, Sam. There's no telling what he'll do."

"I know it's risky," Sam admitted. "But it's the only chance we have. I need to try and negotiate with him, to make him see that this needs to end. Maybe I can get him to let you go, to leave us both alone."

Mike's heart ached. He didn't want her to go, didn't want her anywhere near Tyrell or his men. But deep down, he knew they couldn't keep running. And he knew his wife would not give up till she got her way.

"Sam...," he began, "What if he doesn't agree? What if he wants something more from you?"

Sam took a deep breath. "Then I'll deal with it," she said firmly. "I have to do this, Mike. For both of us."

"Alright," he said quietly. "But please, be careful. I can't lose you, Sam."

Sam nodded, reaching up to cup his face in her hands. "I'll be careful," she promised.

Before she knew it, Sam was staring down at the flip phone those goons had given her. It was the only way to reach Tyrell and try to negotiate Mike's freedom. She wiped her palms on her jeans, took a deep breath, and picked up the phone. It felt cold in her hand as she flipped it open and dialed the only number on the phone that no doubt belonged to Tyrell.

The phone rang twice before it connected. There was a brief silence on the other end, followed by the deep, rough voice of Tyrell.

"Smith, you better have a damn good reason for calling me on this line," Tyrell growled, clearly mistaking her for one of his men. "You know better than to reach out like this. What the hell are you thinking?"

Sam swallowed hard, her voice shaking slightly as she interrupted him. "It's not Smith," she said quickly. "This is Sam. Mike's wife."

There was a brief pause, and when Tyrell spoke again, his tone was colder. "Mrs. Serrano herself, hmm? What are you doing with that phone? And where's Mike?"

Sam took a deep breath, gathering her courage. "Mike's not here. I'm the one who called. I need to talk to you."

"Talk to me about what? What the hell do you want?"

"I want to meet with you, in person. Somewhere private."

Tyrell snorted on the other end of the line, clearly amused. "And why would I agree to that? You think you can just waltz in and demand a meeting with me?"

"I'm not demanding," Sam replied, her voice firm. "I'm asking. I'm willing to negotiate."

Another pause, and then Tyrell sighed. "You've got guts, I'll give you that." he said, a hint of respect in his voice. "Alright, I'll meet with you. But this better be worth my time. If you're wasting it, I won't hesitate to take what I'm owed."

Sam's heart skipped a beat, but she forced herself to stay calm. "It'll be worth it," she promised. "Just tell me when and where."

"There's a warehouse on 34th and Lex. Be there at midnight. And don't even think about bringing anyone with you. This is between you and me."

"I understand," Sam replied, her voice steady. "I'll be there."

The rest of the day passed and soon it was midnight. Sam made her way out of her apartment in the dead of night while Mike was asleep and made her way to the warehouse Tyrell had set up. Her heart pounded in her chest as she approached the large, rusted metal door. She reached the door, and it creaked open as if it had been waiting for her.

The inside of the warehouse was dimly lit. Tyrell was waiting for her near the center of the warehouse, leaning casually against a stack of metal crates. He was dressed in a tailored suit, a weird choice of clothing for this time of night, Sam thought to herself. The look on his face was one of smug amusement and it made Sam uncomfortable.

"You're punctual. I like that," Tyrell said with a smirk. "It shows you're serious."

"I am," Sam replied. She stopped a few feet away from him. "Let's get straight to it. What will it take for you to leave Mike alone?"

Tyrell chuckled, a low, mocking sound. "Straight to the point, huh? I respect that. Look honey, your husband owes me a lot of money, and I don't see how you're going to change that. What exactly do you have to negotiate with?"

"I'm willing to buy his freedom," she said, "I'll do whatever it takes to get you to leave him alone. I don't care if I have to work or anything, just leave my husband alone."

There was a lone pause as Tyrell pondered the woman in front of him. "I'm not the kind of man that gives second chances, Sam but I happen to know that you're willing to go the extra mile. My boys told me all about what happened back at your place."

Sam felt her cheeks flush with embarrassment. She hadn't expected Tyrell to know about what had transpired with his men, let alone bring it up so casually.

"What does that have to do with anything?" she demanded. "I did what I had to do to protect Mike. That's all that matters."

Tyrell pushed himself off the crates and took a step closer to her, "Oh, it has everything to do with this. You see, Sam, you've already shown me how far you're willing to go. You've proven you're desperate enough to do whatever it takes. That gives me all the leverage I need."

Sam's heart sank "What do you want from me, Tyrell?" she asked, her voice trembling slightly. "I'm here to negotiate Mike's freedom. Just tell me what it'll take."

Tyrell grinned. "It's simple," he said, "I'll let your husband go, but only if you agree to become my property for a while."

Sam's eyes widened in shock, her breath catching in her throat. She couldn't believe what she was hearing. "Your... property?" she echoed.

Tyrell nodded. "That's right. You'll belong to me. You'll do whatever I say, whenever I say it. And in return, I'll make sure Mike walks away from all this unscathed."

"You said you were willing to do whatever it took. You made a big show about it, coming here and making demands in my territory. So put your money where your mouth is and protect your darling husband."

Sam's mind raced. The idea of becoming Tyrell's property, of submitting to his control, was repulsive. But as much as she wanted to scream at him, to tell him where he could shove his twisted offer up his black ass, she knew she didn't have much of a choice. Mike's life was on the line, and Tyrell held all the power.

"Fine," she whispered, her voice breaking. "I'll do it. Just... just promise me you'll leave Mike alone."

"You have my word," Tyrell said smoothly, reaching out to caress her cheek. "Welcome to your new life, Sam."

CHAPTER NINETEEN: Bound and Blindfolded

After promising herself to Tyrell, he wasted no time in showing her what he meant about making her his property. As soon as she told him that she would be his, he was leading her to his car, ready to whisk her away to his penthouse.

"Where are we going?" Sam asked, as he opened the door for her to make her way inside.

Tyrell got into the driver seat and started the car. He turned towards her and gave her a soft smile, the first of its kind since she started talking to him. "We are going to make good on our little arrangement, my dear."

Sam's heart pounded in her chest as she sat in the passenger seat of Tyrell's sleek black car. Tyrell suddenly reached over and took something out of the glove box in front of Sam.

"Put this on," Tyrell said, his voice commanding. He handed her a black silk blindfold. He locked eyes with her as if he was daring her to refuse.

Sam hesitated, staring at the blindfold in front of her. "Why do I need to wear this?" she asked.

Tyrell leaned closer, his breath warm against her ear. "Because I want you to. Do you really want to question me right now, Sam?"

The subtle threat had a dual effect on her, it sent a shiver of terror down her spine but it also gave her goosebumps, the kind that could only come from arousal. She knew she didn't have a choice in the matter but instead of making her feel completely helpless, she also felt strangely turned on.

With shaky hands, she tied the blindfold around her eyes, plunging herself into darkness.

The car started moving, and Sam's sense of direction was immediately thrown off thanks to the blindfold. The hum of the engine and the occasional bump in the road were the only indications that they were moving.

Finally, the car came to a stop. Sam heard the soft click of Tyrell's seatbelt, then the sound of his door opening and closing. A moment later, her door swung open, and Tyrell's hand gripped her arm firmly, guiding her out of the car.

"Careful now," he murmured, whispering against her ear as gently as his voice could go. His voice sounded smooth at this moment, was this because of the blindfold?

Tyrell kept her blindfolded as they walked, his hand never leaving her arm. Finally, they stopped and Sam could hear the creak of a door opening, followed by Tyrell gently pushing her forward.

No doubt they had entered a room, and she could smell the faint hint of lavender and something else that she couldn't quite place, it smelt similar to freshly washed silk.

Tyrell leaned closer and licked behind her ears with his tongue. "Don't take it off, your blindfold." Tyrell commanded as if reading her mind. "Not until I say so."

Sam nodded, her heart racing. She reached out her hands but there was nothing for her to grasp. He was completely in control of this situation and it made her feel incredibly vulnerable.

Tyrell suddenly put his hands on her shoulders, they were firm yes but they weren't harsh. It shook Sam as she did not expect any sort of gentility from Tyrell but she welcomed it. His touch was possessive and he slowly undressed her, letting each item of clothing fall to the floor.

The way he took the time to slip each item off her body, it was almost reverential. It made Sam feel honored, in a way she hadn't felt with Jay, Andre or even her husband.

"Do you trust me, Sam?" He asked against her ear as he dropped a kiss on her neck.

Sam scoffed. "Trust you? I don't exactly have the privilege to do that, do I?"

Tyrell chuckled loudly. "Good answer."

He slowly walked her over to the bed, his hands on her waist, trailing downwards till they cupped her ass. He smirked. "Damn, no way Mike's handling all that."

He pressed her down to the mattress and Sam could feel the silk sheets against her skin. Her body was tense, as it should be when it was in the presence of a man like Tyrell. She forced herself to relax, though; after all, the whole point of this was to submit to Tyrell's control.

Tyrell climbed in beside her, his hands roaming her body. Sam gasped when his hands cupped her breasts before he pinched her nipples between his fingers. Somehow the fact that she couldn't see only heightened her other senses so she felt everything. From the way he rolled her nipple between his fingers and the way his hand roamed all over her body.

"Right now Sam, you belong to me." He said, his breath hot against her skin. "I'm going to show you exactly what that means." His lips found her neck and he trailed hot kisses down to her collarbone then down past her navel to her vulva.

He finally settled himself between her thighs, causing her to shiver in anticipation. He parted her legs gently then she felt his warm breath against her skin.

His lips brushed her inner thighs and she gasped, bucking upwards in excitement. He took his time to explore her, pressing his tongue against her clit with pressure that gradually became firmer and more insistent.

His hands gripped her hips, holding her steady as his mouth worked wonders on her. She tangled her fingers into his hair when he began sucking on her clit lightly. She could feel herself getting overwhelmed and the pressure began to build within her.

His rhythm became more urgent and soon she had no choice but to cum right into his mouth. He didn't pull away immediately, instead let her ride her orgasm out. Only when she had come down from her high did he pull away, kiss up her body and then claim her lips. She could taste herself on him.

Tyrell moved quickly and before Sam knew what was happening, he had flipped her over and propped her up such that she was on her knees with her ass facing him, doggy-style.

She still couldn't see anything, she could only feel and she felt him use his dickhead to stroke her now very sensitive clitoris.

"I'm about to fuck the shit out of you." He said, groaning as he pushed himself into her. He grabbed her hips and gave a powerful thrust that made her cry out and hold onto the sheets. He filled her up completely and she could tell he was big from the way her pussy tingled as he made his way in.

He set a fast pace, driving into her without a care in a way that came off as possessive. Every thrust filled her with pleasure and she couldn't help but moan as he drove himself into her over and over again.

Her breath came out ragged as he moved inside her, the sound of his thighs slapping against her ass filled the room. His grip on her hips were firm and she could hear his own ragged breaths, clearly turned on by her body.

He leaned over her until she could feel his breath hot against her ear. "You feel so fucking good." he groaned, emphasizing his words with a several deep thrusts that sent waves of pleasure into her.

His hands slid up her spine and he reached for her hair, pulling her head back slightly. He angled his hips so his thrusts hit just the right spot over and over again. She could feel the tension in her body get tighter, meaning she was close.

But he was far from done with her.

CHAPTER TWENTY:
Unfinished Business

Tyrell was still buried deep inside of her. He kept his grip on her hips as he pulled out slowly, ever so slowly. It was like he was trying to tease her with the friction he was making. He gave her a small moment to catch her breath before he pulled her closer to him by her hips. He leaned over and whispered in her ear:

"On your back," he commanded, his voice low.

Sam knew that there was no point in resisting this man. So, turning over, Sam lay on her back. Tyrell wasted no time. He spread her legs wide, positioning himself between her thighs, and thrust back into her. The new angle sent shocks of pleasure through her, and her back arched off the bed as she moaned.

He set a slower, deliberate rhythm this time, pulling out nearly all the way before slamming back into her, making her toes curl.

"Fuck, Tyrell" she gasped, her nails digging into the sheets as her body writhed beneath him. He looked down at her intensely, he was enjoying watching her face contort from all the pleasure that he was giving her.

He leaned forward and took her lips into a harsh kiss, one that could leave a bruise if he pulled away. His hand slid between their bodies and found her clit, his fingers began to move in small circles around it. They worked in sync with his thrusts and the combination of the sensation was sending Sam over the edge.

Her body was shaking, she could feel herself getting closer. Tyrell could sense that she was getting close so he pulled back suddenly and flipped her onto her side.

Sam was taken aback by his sudden gesture and equally surprised by how nimble she was after all of these years. He was making her feel like a young woman again, the way he was flinging her around. He grabbed her legs and raised them as high as he could go as he positioned himself behind her.

This new position allowed him to drive even deeper into her, and Sam let out a loud moan as he pounded into her. His hand reached out and grabbed unto a tit, squeezing and pulling on her nipples as he buried himself to the hilt. The sound of skin slapping against skin grew louder in the room.

"You take me so fucking well," he groaned, "that's good."

Somehow his praise made Sam feel really good. If a man like this could tell her that she's good then maybe she was. He slammed into her relentlessly and Sam's head fell back.

She felt her orgasm building again but Tyrell wasn't slowing down. His pace quickened, his thrusts growing more erratic as he chased his release. Sam grew brazen and reached behind her, gripping his thigh, urging him. When he thrusted in one more time, her orgasm crashed over her like a tidal wave.

Her body clenched around him and her breath hitched as she came hard, her entire body shaking. Tyrell cursed under his breath and gripped her hips tighter as he gave four more deep thrusts then let out a long moan before pulling out and coming all over the place.

They stayed still for a moment, the sweat from their bodies falling onto the bed. Sam's chest heaved and her head was foggy from pleasure.

Tyrell stood up from the bed, still breathing hard, as he took his pants off his floor and began to get dressed. Sam remained in bed, unsure of what to do now.

"You're free to go," Tyrell said, his voice now cold once again. He glanced at her. "You did what you came here for."

Sam slowly got up from the bed, searching for her clothes, which were scattered all over the room. Tyrell didn't say anything else as she got dressed. He simply nodded towards the door, and she walked out of the room.

When she got out, she sat on the ground for a moment, her mind racing.

The guilt hit her first. She had done this for Mike, to save him from Tyrell and the life he had gotten tangled in. But even so, it felt wrong. This wasn't the same as her encounters with Andre or the others. Back then, it was consensual between her and Mike. He had known about it, had wanted it.

But this... this was different.

How had she gotten here? Her body still hummed with the lingering bliss of what had just happened. It scared her, how much she had enjoyed it. But she couldn't ignore the truth, it wasn't supposed to feel this good. Not like this, not with someone outside of the lifestyle she had entered with Mike's approval or someone who brought so much danger into their lives.

She stood up and started walking. She was doing this for her husband, she reminded herself, to free him from the hold Tyrell had over him. But even as she repeated that, it didn't feel justified.

By the time she got home, she found Mike in their bedroom. He asked her where she was coming from but she couldn't answer. She told him that she needed some rest and he let her be.

The next day, Mike woke up earlier than Sam then went to retrieve some mail. When he opened the door he found a package on his doorstep with a note attached. He looked around to see if anyone who had dropped it was close by. When he didn't see anybody, he brought it into the house.

He removed the note from the package and read it, his blood running cold as. he did so.

"Heard you liked watching your wife fuck big black men. Watch this."

Frantically, he opened the package and in it he found a USB. Rushing to his bedroom and trying not to wake Sam up, he inserted the USB into their computer and to his shock, it was a video of Tyrell taking his wife from behind.

Mike stood there, completely taken aback at what he was seeing. What was this about? When did this happen? He thought to himself.

"Mike," He heard a voice behind him say. He turned around to see his wife looking at him with guilt. "Mike, I can explain."

What explanation could she possibly give that would justify her sleeping with the man that was ruining his life?

THE END OF BOOK 3

CHAPTER TWENTY-ONE:
Reawakened Desires

Sam could feel her stomach tightening as she watched the screen in front of the both of them, the video playing in slow motion. Tyrell has recorded them and she had no idea. She looked at Mike who was still watching and rewinding the tape, unsure of what to say.

Eventually, he paused the video and turned to look at her? "How long has this been going on?" he asked, his voice coming out a little choked. "How long were you planning on keeping this from me?"

"Look, I can explain." Sam started, swallowing slightly. "I can explain, I wasn't trying to hide it. I just knew that I had to do this for you and Tyrell gave me this proposal that if I slept with him he would wipe your debt clean."

"That's not how shit like this work Sam." Mike said, raising his voice slightly. "You don't make deals with the devil, you only end up burned. Tyrell just wanted to hit and quit, I doubt that he had any intentions of letting me go."

"Well what choice did I have? You're the one who got involved with a drug dealer yet you're giving me problems trying to fix the issue you made?"

"Oh, that's what you're using to make yourself feel better? You did this for me? I don't buy it. I think you're just horny for some BBC again."

"Excuse me?!" Sam shouted, getting to her feet. "Where do you get off talking to me like that?"

Mike bit his lip, regretting his words. He was annoyed, yes but that wasn't a reason to throw shade at her lifestyle. After all, wasn't he involved in it as well? He didn't know how to feel though, the thought of her sleeping with someone else was one thing but did that person have to be his boss? And he knew Tyrell well enough to know that even if she did what he said, the likelihood of him being free was very low.

Mike sighed and sat down on the bed, burying his hands in his hands. "I appreciate what you were trying to do and I'm sorry for putting us in this situation. I'm just worried about you getting involved with Tyrell, that's all."

Sam took a seat besides her husband. "I understand what you mean but maybe we can hope for the best? You always say that Tyrell is a man of his words."

"He is but I also know that he likes to screw people over and apparently he has a thing for screwing my wife now. This just doesn't feel like a solution, if anything it feels like we're only digging ourselves deeper."

"So what do we do?" Sam asked.

"I think you need to tell him that it's over, Sam." His tone was softer now, like he was pleasing with her. "If this was really for me then you're done now. So we can move on."

"Is it really that easy?" Sam asked, reaching for her phone where Tyrell's contact information was stored.

"I don't know, but there's only one way to find out."

Sam sighed and looked at her phone. She wanted to listen to her husband, she really did but what would that mean for her and what she wanted? Yes, she did this for him but she couldn't deny how good it felt to be with Tyrell. He dominated her, pounded her over and over until she felt like she couldn't take it anymore. He was a bad guy no doubt but why did he have to fuck so good?

"I guess I have no choice." She says, opening her phone up and heading to her messages to draft a text to send to Tyrell.

Just at that moment, her phone made a buzzing noise, interrupting the silence of the room. Sam felt her heart drop as she saw the message, it was from Tyrell.

"Tomorrow night. My place. We aren't done yet."

Her hand tightened around the phone. The words were simple enough but she could hear his voice behind them, commanding and authoritative. She knew what he was capable of and she knew exactly what he wanted. Could she resist?

"Who is it?" Mike's voice cut through her thoughts but she quickly put the phone away, hoping her guilt didn't show on her face.

"No one," she replied, avoiding his gaze.

Mike sighed, his expression weary. "Sam, if you want to keep our marriage together, you need to stop this. Whatever thrill you're getting out of this, I can't do it. I'm asking you. End it with him…for good."

She nodded, forcing a smile to put him at ease. "I will. I promise."

But as she lay in bed that night, staring up at the ceiling, she couldn't help but think about Tyrell's message. '*We're not done yet*'.

She thought back to when last they hooked up and the way he had made her feel. She hadn't felt anything like that in a very long time and as she drifted off to sleep, only one thought was on her mind.

Tyrell wasn't done with her and she wasn't done with him either.

The next day, Sam pretended to oversleep and waited for her husband to leave the house before she got up to start getting ready to go meet Tyrell. She waited in silence, listening for the faint sound of the garage door closing. As soon as she heard Mike's car pull out of the driveway, she quickly grabbed her coat and purse, slipping out the door and into her car before she could talk herself out of it. She knew she should be staying home and honoring her promise to Mike but all she could think about was being under Tyrell again.

A couple of minutes later, she was in front of Tyrell's building, guarded by hidden security with the sharpest eyes. One of them nodded and escorts her in, barely speaking as they led her up to Tyrell's apartment. The suite was just as lavish as she remembere, sleek leather, floor-to-ceiling windows and artwork that must have cost more than her entire house.

They leave her alone in a waiting area, offering nothing more than a curt nod to her. She glances around the room and it was then she realized that she had no control over this situation or any power over it either.

Minutes later, she heard footsteps and turned just as Tyrell entered. He looked as composed as ever, in his tailored suit.

"Sam," he greeted her, a smirk tugging at the corner of his mouth. "Right on time."

She straightened, immediately getting to the point. "You sent that video to Mike without my consent," she said, keeping her voice as steady as she could. "Why would you do that?"

Tyrell's smirk widened,. "Why do you care?" he asked, his voice smooth and unbothered, as if her question barely registered to him.

"Because it's... it's not okay," she stammered, finding her confidence slipping under his gaze. "I thought this was supposed to be between us, I was doing that to help my husband out but then sending it to him, that wasn't part of the deal."

Tyrell laughed. "The deal? You still think this is about what you want?"

Sam's mouth opened and she began making a staggering defense on why what he did wasn't okay. Tyrell didn't give her the chance to get into it though, before she knew what was happening, he unbuckled his pants, crossed the room, slipped his dick out and shoved it into her mouth before she could protest.

He gripped her chin, tilting her face towards him as he used the head to trace the corner of her lips then shove back into her mouth again.

"Let's get one thing straight," he said as his fingers held her jaw in place. "I didn't call you here to talk about what you want, Sam."

All she could taste was the strong, musky flavor of him. He held on to her jaw, guiding her head up and dow his shaft when he noticed that she was making no effort to suck on him by herself.

"Now," Tyrell continued. "Why don't you show me that you understand."

Sam sat there, his cock in between her lips, feeling both humiliated and aroused. She used her tongue to tentatively lick the head and flushed with warmth when she saw Tyrell close his eyes slightly with pleasure.

He may have most of the control here but she still had some tricks to take the power back. She reached out to him and grabbed the shaft, stroking it gently as she made a sucking motion with her lips.

"Good girl," he murmured. He stepped back, turning toward the hall, gesturing for her to follow him into his bedroom. Now she knew this was a dangerous game but still she followed Tyrell down the dimly lit hall and into his bedroom.

"Let's see if you remember why you're here," he said, taking off the rest of his clothes.

There was no turning back now.

CHAPTER TWENTY-TWO:
Strange Loyalty

Tyrell stood in front of her, completely naked and with his dick erect, calling her to him. Sam could see it pulsing, the top of the head glistening with precum, precum that she feels an intense urge to lick off.

She lifted her head up to look at him but found that she was unable to hold his gaze. He was staring at her intensely, in a way that almost made her breathless.

"On your knees," he commanded her, pointing his fingers downward to indicate that he wanted her in front of his dick.

Sam's heart was pounding hard as she dropped down in front of Tyrell, feeling the cold floor beneath her knees. She kept her face down but then he tilted her face up, telling her to "Look at me." he ordered.
He held onto his dick and brought it in front of her face once again, tapping her lips with it slightly. "Open," he ordered and Sam obeyed, parting her lips as he leaned forward and slid his dick between her lips with a deliberate slowness that caused him to groan out loud.

She closed her lips around it, feeling the precum on the tip of her tongue. Tyrell let out a small gasp then smirked. "Show me, I want to see just how much you enjoy this."

Sam began to suck gently at first then swirled her tongue around it, pressing her lips tightly around the piece of candy. More precum began to leak out of it and this caused her to increase the intensity of her movement. She wanted to see Tyrell begging in front of her, lost in the pleasure that she was giving him.

"Good girl," he groaned, titling his head back as he savored what she did to him.

She sucked his cock a bit deeper into her mouth, tilting her head back just slightly, letting him see the way she worked her mouth around it. He let out a long, strained groan as he shoved it into her mouth, hitting the back of her throat.

"Don't stop," he whispered, thrusting it into her mouth over and over again. "That's right, take your time. Don't stop."

Sam's cheeks were burning at this point but she obeyed, letting her tongue trace along the shaft as she sucked on. Tyrell was thrusting faster now and she was finding it hard to keep up. He grabbed her head, gripping her hair and shoving his dick deeper into her mouth, causing her to gag on it.

She ran her tongue along the head of his dick and Tyrell let out a long, strained groan as he shoved his dick into her mouth one last time, spraying the back of her throat with his cum.

"Fuckkkk," he groaned. "Take my cum, white bitch." He said, stroking his dick into her mouth slowly as he came in it.

"See?" he murmured, "I knew you could be... do it."

Sam swallowed his cum, his dick still in her mouth. She wasn't sure what she liked most about this interaction, whether it was the control that he held over

"Good," he said. "Now that I've seen you follow directions, let's see how you handle the rest."

With one last, lingering look, he took his dick out of her mouth, now soft and still dripping a little bit of cum.

He released her from his grip, stepping back just enough to observe her as she straightened. She could tell by his expression that she'd pleased him. Tyrell reached down, taking her by the hand and pulling her up to her feet. Without a word, he led her toward the bed. She followed him, her heart racing as he held onto her hand.

When they reached the edge of the bed, he stopped, turning to face her. He placed his hands on her shoulders, guiding her backward until she felt the mattress behind her. He straddled her, then slowly started taking off all her clothes until she was left in nothing but her bra.

"Pink lace...and you were acting like you didn't want this." He said, chuckling.

"You came here to satisfy me," he said. "And I'm not done with you yet."

He leaned into her, his hands trailing down her side as he felt up her body. She held her breath as she felt his touch tracing over her skin. He leaned down and brushed his lips against her neck. His hands gripped her waist tight and she arched underneath him, as he got between her thighs and buried himself into her.

"Tell me you want this," he whispered, sighing as he thrusted into her slowly.

"I... I want this," she replied, as his thrusts sent wave after wave of pleasure into her.

"Good," he said. "Now, let's see if you can keep up."

Tyrell increased the intensity of his thrusts, driving himself into Sam until she was absolutely breathless. He wrapped her legs around him, which caused him to go deeper into her.

The sound of their bodies slapping against each other filled the room. Sam was so wet that he couldn't resist leaning over and pounding into her repeatedly. Sam could feel her pulse quickening as he gripped unto her. He leaned down and brushed his lips against her neck and she let out a shaky breath, unable to hide her reaction as his mouth found her most sensitive spot under her ear.

A low hum of satisfaction came from his throat when he felt her tremble beneath him, his fingers pressing firmly into her hips. He buries his hands into her hair, pulling her head back just enough to expose her neck as he moved writhing her deeper, his thrusts more relentless.

"You can take it, can't you?" he taunted, his voice a low growl.

"Yes," she gasped, barely able to form any words as he drove her to the edge. She couldn't think any coherent thoughts, all that was in her mind was how good he was making her feel.
He smirked to himself when he noticed the effect he was having on her. It was enough to drive him over the edge and it did. Sam could feel him shuddering as he got closer and closer, his grip on her tightening and his breaths becoming more shallow until he couldn't take it anymore and he pulled out quickly, cumming all over the mattress.

Before he had let her cum before he did, this time it was all about him. It was like he was trying to send Sam a message, a message that said 'he held all the cards, not her.'

He let out a satisfied sigh then headed to the en-suite bathroom not too far from the bed. He came out and threw a towel her way to clean herself up with. She took it with thanks but could only lay there to catch her breath, her body still buzzing from the aftershocks.

She sat up then smoothed the towel all over herself. She didn't know if she was trying to erase the evidence of what just happened so Mike would be none the wiser when she got back home. She looked in Tyrell's direction, watching as he relieved against the pillows, his dick soft by this point.
When she was finally able to steady her breathing, she mustered up the courage to ask the question that had been lingering at the back of her mind. "So after this, does this mean that we're done? Does this

mean that Mike's debt is clear? Am I free to go? I'm not sure how long I can keep doing this."

Tyrell has a smirk on his face and he took a deep breath before he answered. "Done?" He repeated the word as if he were tasting it. Sam swallowed, unsure of what his response would be. It was so hard to predict this man.

Tyrell leaned forward, his eyes narrowing as he looked her over. "You'll be done, Sam," he began, "when I decide I've had enough. When I'm ready to let you go, and not a moment before."

A chill ran down her spine at that moment and she could feel anxiety rising in her chest. Her husband had been right, nothing she did would fix this problem. Tyrell would just keep using her and using her until he got tired of her. How foolish of her to believe that she had anything valuable to offer this man that would make him forget the fact that Mike owed him thousands of dollars.

Her fingers tightened around the towel as she fought to maintain her composure. "I thought we had a deal," she murmured, her voice faint yet hoping that he might reconsider.

He tilted his head, a slight smile on his lips as he watched her struggle to assert herself. "We do, Sam. And I intend to keep my end of it. But remember, you came to me. You wanted this arrangement, and now you'll finish it on my terms."

Sam swallowed, she wanted to protest but he was right. She wanted this and she got exactly what she was looking for.

CHAPTER TWENTY-THREE: Revelations

Mike was at the kitchen table, fingers clenched around his phone as the video loaded. He didn't know what to expect when the anonymous message pinged onto his screen. His gut told him it was another recording from Tyrell, another twisted reminder that he still wasn't free from the man's control, that Tyrell still had Sam wrapped around his finger but he couldn't be sure. Not until he opened it.

The video started to play and Mike's breath caught as he saw Sam, his wife, kneeling in front of Tyrell and sucking on his dick. Her face was turned toward the camera, although she was clearly oblivious to its presence. He watched, anger and shame burning through him as Tyrell's hands roamed over her, grabbing her hair, claiming her, treating her as if she were his.

"Damn it," he muttered under his breath, hitting pause but unable to look away. Why was Tyrell doing this? Why send these to him, was it just a power play, a way to show Mike who was really in control?

The sound of Sam's laughter drifted through from the other room, and Mike felt his anger twist into confusion. She had promised him she'd end things, that this entire arrangement was over. Yet here she was, caught on camera again, in Tyrell's bed.

When he confronted her last time, she'd looked at him with wide, guilt-ridden eyes, "It was for you," she'd told him, voice trembling. "I only did it to protect you."

And he'd believed her. At least, he had wanted to believe her. But seeing her like this, caught on video made him doubt everything.

He heard footsteps approaching and quickly locked his phone, shoving it into his pocket just as Sam walked into the kitchen. She smiled at him, reaching for a coffee mug, her face calm and almost carefree. It was as if she had no idea what he'd just seen.

"Morning," she said, pouring coffee and leaning against the counter. "You're up early."

Mike's gaze became sharp all of a sudden. He couldn't keep the suspicion from his face. "Couldn't sleep," he muttered, the edge in his tone unmistakable. He watched her carefully, looking for any hint of guilt, any sign that she knew what he had just seen.

Sam took a sip of her coffee, glancing at him over the rim of her mug. "Are you all right?" she asked, her brow creasing slightly.

"Just... got a lot on my mind." He forced himself to look away. He hated this feeling, it's as if Tyrell had invaded their lives, placing a wedge between him and Sam that he couldn't remove. And it was all his fault.

"I was thinking," he began carefully, trying to keep his voice steady, "about what you said... that you'd stopped everything with Tyrell."

Sam's face got tight, her eyes darting away for a fraction of a second. It was so subtle but Mike caught it.

"Of course I did," she replied, her voice defensive. "You know that."

"Right," he replied, barely able to keep the bitterness from his voice. "So if he... I don't know, tried to reach out to you again, you'd tell me. Right?"

She looked at him, a little too quickly, her smile tight. "Yes, Mike. I would tell you."

The lie twisted in his chest, making it hard to breathe. He wasn't sure if he wanted to call her out on it now, to ask her outright why she was still sneaking around or if he wanted to let it slide, to keep the peace a little longer.

But then his phone buzzed again in his pocket, the vibration cutting through the silence between them. He didn't pull it out, he didn't have to. He already knew what it would be.

Sam looked at him, brow furrowing. "You going to get that?"

He shook his head. "No. It can wait."

She nodded, though he could see the question in her eyes. But she didn't press him and a part of him was grateful for that. He wasn't sure he could keep it together if she did.

As she left the room, he pulled out his phone, his hands shaking slightly as he checked the notification. Another video, just like before. Another message from Tyrell, taunting him with the knowledge that Sam was still under his thumb.

He pressed play again, his heart pounding as he watched the scene unfold. Part of him couldn't look away. Part of him was drawn in, watching Tyrell take control of Sam, watching the way she responded, the way she surrendered.

And in that moment, Mike realized he wasn't sure what angered him more, the fact that Sam was lying to him or the fact that some dark part of him couldn't help but watch.
Mike stood there with his phone tightly gripped in his hands. All he could do was glare at the screen as he watched this man thrust into his wife over and over again.

As the video continued, Tyrell's hands moved over Sam and he watched his wife's face flush with pleasure, her body responding openly. She looked lost in the moment, by the way Tyrell touched her. And while Mike wanted to look away, he knew that his body wanted him to keep watching.

"What am I doing?" he muttered to himself as his eyes followed Tyrell's movements, his grip on Sam. It was different, so different from how Mike would touch her. Where Mike was gentle with Sam, not wanting to hurt her. Tyrell took whatever he wanted without caring how she felt.

Somehow knowing that there was a side to his wife that he didn't know who to bring out made a wave of heat pass through him and his pulse quickened even as Tyrell increased the speed of his thrusts.

The conflicting emotions in his chest seemed to fight to be the dominant feeling, his anger fading as he realized he was... excited. In ways he hadn't felt in a long time since well Jay.

Glancing around the room to make sure Sam wasn't nearby, he quietly snuck down the hallway, slipping into the guest bathroom and locking the door behind him. His fingers shook slightly as he set his phone on the counter, leaning over the sink and staring down at the screen, the heat in his dick intensifying.

"Damn it," he muttered, feeling shame mix with the rush of arousal. He pressed play again and he buried his hand into his pants, pulling his dick out. It was red, erect and already leaking precum. He pressed play again and began stroking his penis in rhythm with the way Tyrell was pounding into Sam. His breathing became shallow, almost like his hand was moving on its own.

The sound of Sam's moans filled his mind, she was moaning in a way that she had never with him. It made him feel so turned on somehow, the emasculation of it all.

As he gave in to the need, the images of Sam's face, her body arching under Tyrell's touch, filled his mind, and the intensity of his response shocked him. His dick jerked as he stroked it harder and harder, practically turning red from all the friction. The pleasure grew, overtaking him, building quickly as he lost himself in the sounds, the sight and everything.

Pretty soon he felt a tightening in his stomach and pleasure washed over him as he came into the sink. He let out a quiet sigh, not wanting Sam to hear what was going on.

He stood there for a moment, eyes closed, catching breath. He rested his hands on the sink as he struggled to pull himself back from the edge. He glanced down at the phone, still paused on the video, and felt his stomach twist again but not from pleasure this time.

"What's wrong with me?" he whispered, shaking his head. He couldn't believe he'd given in to that impulse, couldn't believe that something like this had gotten to him so deeply. The shame settled heavily in his chest, mixing with the frustration he was feeling.

He shut off the phone, the silence of the room even louder now that the video was gone. As he leaned over the sink, he could still see her face in his mind and he hated himself a little for it.

The thought of facing Sam now...she had no idea that he'd received the videos or how they affected him and he wasn't sure he wanted her to know.

Running a hand through his hair, he took a deep breath. He knew that eventually he'd have to confront her about this whole thing but then he began to think, did he have to? Couldn't he just let the sleeping dogs lie?

And besides for whatever misguided reason, his wife was doing this for him. He never would have been in this mess if he hadn't gotten involved with the wrong crowd. So can he really blame his wife for looking after him especially after he kept things from her in that way.

He splashed cold water on his face and it grounded him. He would have to confront all of these emotions much later, right now he could just be grateful he wasn't in anymore danger.

CHAPTER TWENTY-FOUR:
Rekindling the Thrill

Sam's hands shook as she stared at the message on her husband's phone. She couldn't believe it, Tyrell was doing it again. He sent videos of them to Mike's phone again!

She knew he did this before but why would he do it again? What was he gaining out of it? Why did he keep doing this? She felt exposed and betrayed again but what could she expect from a drug dealer? She couldn't let this keep happening, she had to put a stop to it right now.

It didn't take long for her to find herself back at Tyrell's lavish mansion. The guards let her in without a word, clearly used to her by now but Sam stormed past them without a glance, driven by anger and anxiety. Tyrell was seated on a sleek leather couch in the waiting area, his attention seemingly elsewhere as she entered but then a faint smirk curled on his lips as he looked up and met her staring at him.

"Back so soon?" he drawled, amusement in his eyes. "Didn't expect to see you again so quickly."

Sam clenched her fists, barely holding back her anger. "What are you doing, Tyrell?" she demanded. "Sending those videos to Mike? Again? That's not fair. You're crossing a line and you know it."

He chuckled, leaning back against the couch with a casualness that only made her more frustrated. "Fair?" he repeated, arching a brow. "Sam, we're far past fair here. I don't owe you or Mike anything. I've been more than generous, given everything he owes me."

"But this is different," she shot back, her voice filled with desperation. "This is personal. You're deliberately trying to humiliate him, humiliate me."

Tyrell's smirk only deepened. "Maybe," he said smoothly. "Or maybe I'm just reminding him of the cost of his choices. Besides, you weren't complaining before. You seemed pretty eager to come back every time."

Sam's face flushed with embarrassment and anger. "That's not the point, Tyrell," she said quietly, her voice shaking slightly. "This, this isn't ethical. What you're doing, it's manipulative."

He shrugged, unbothered by her accusation. "Ethics are for people who don't hold all the cards. But," he continued, tilting his head as if considering her, "I'm feeling generous today. Maybe I'll wipe Mike's debt and we can call it even."

All of Mike's debt, gone? She should have felt relieved, grateful even. This was the end of their troubles, the escape they'd been waiting for. But then reality sank in, she felt disappointment. If Tyrell cleared the debt, then... this strange, reckless arrangement with him would end.

Seeing her hesitate, Tyrell's smile grew. "What's wrong, Sam? Not the reaction I was expecting. Shouldn't you be grateful?"

She forced herself to look away, trying to gather her thoughts. "Of course I'm grateful," she replied. "It's just... a lot to process." She thought of Mike, the relief he'd feel if he knew Tyrell's threats were finally over. He'd been so anxious, so weighed down by the debt and now he could breathe easy. She knew that was what mattered most, but somehow, the finality of it left her feeling unsettled.

"Take it or leave it," Tyrell said coolly, watching her closely. "I'm not offering again."

Sam swallowed, fighting the strange pang in her chest. She nodded, forcing herself to focus on what this meant for her family. "Fine. We'll take it," she replied. "Just stop sending those videos. You've done enough."

Tyrell raised his hands in a mock gesture of surrender. "Consider it done." He leaned forward. "But let's be clear, Sam, this doesn't mean I'm done with you. I let you go when I decide to. Understood?"

Sam met his gaze. "As long as Mike's debt is cleared, that's all that matters to me." She turned to leave, feeling the weight of his eyes on her back but she kept her head high, refusing to let him see her uncertainty.

Back home, she told Mike the news and he stared at her, stunned. "All of it?" he repeated, his voice filled with disbelief and relief. "We're... we're finally free of him?"

"Yes," Sam replied, forcing a smile. "It's over."

He exhaled, closing his eyes as if a massive weight had just lifted from his shoulders. "This is it, Sam. We can finally move on."

She nodded, willing herself to feel the same relief he felt but then there was an odd emptiness in her. She pushed it aside, knowing that Mike needed his peace about this more than anything. For him, this was a fresh start. She just had to let go of everything and believe that too.

She lay in bed that night, staring up at the ceiling, her mind restless despite the late hour. Tyrell's decision to end things had left her feeling conflicted. Part of her had been relieved when he'd offered to clear Mike's debt, thinking this would finally bring peace. Yet she couldn't shake the emptiness in her chest.

Tyrell had brought her so much pleasure. Could she really give all of that up?

Beside her, Mike stirred, glancing over and noticing the distant look on her face. "You okay?" he asked,

Sam hesitated, wondering how to even begin explaining this. "Yeah... I guess." She turned onto her side, facing him. "It's just... I don't know. Everything feels different now. Going back to normal just seems strange."

He sighed, reaching over to brush a strand of hair from her face. "Look, Sam, we've been through a lot. Maybe it'll just take some time to get used to things being... simple again."

She bit her lip, hesitating. "It's not just that. I mean, after everything, it's hard to pretend things haven't changed. Tyrell... he showed me something I didn't even realize I wanted. Or needed. I don't think I can just go back to how things were before." She paused, gathering her thoughts. "It's like, now that I've... experienced that, I don't know if I can settle back into what we had."

Mike was quiet, his brow furrowed as he processed her words. "Are you saying..." He cleared his throat, glancing away briefly before meeting her gaze again. "You're saying you want more of... that? Even if it's not with him? That dangerous kind of toxic sex?"

She nodded slowly. "Yeah something like that. We've ended things with all these other people and I just know I'm not ready to go back to normal now.."

Mike exhaled, rubbing the back of his neck. "I get it, Sam. Really, I do. And as much as it's tough for me to admit, I know things changed for both of us." He looked back at her, his expression softer now. "Maybe we don't have to go back to the way things were. Maybe we don't have to give up on this lifestlye now that Tyrell is gone."

Sam looked at him, surprised. "You mean...?"

He shrugged, a small smile tugging at his lips. "We tried it before, right? With Jay, Andre. And I'll admit, there was something kind of... exciting about it. Maybe we could look online again, see if we can find someone who fits what you're looking for. Together."

Sam's pulse quickened at the suggestion, a thrill running through her at the thought. "You'd really be okay with that?"

He chuckled, shaking his head slightly. "Okay might be pushing it, I'm still recovering from the whole Tyrell thing but I liked parts of it when we did it last time. And I want to make you happy and if this is part of it, I think I can get there. As long as we're doing it together."

She smiled, feeling a warmth spread through her. "Okay, then. Let's... let's give it a try."

Over the next few days, they set up dusted off their laptop and reactivated their dormant profiles together, crafting a message that felt genuine but also hinted at their interests. It was so strange being back here, scrolling through profiles and mooming for couples that shared the same open-minded as they did. They laughed, hesitated, and debated over potential matches, the whole experience bringing a lightheartedness she hadn't felt in a long time with her husband. It was nice, feeling completely different from all the drama Tyrell brought.

Finally, they received a message from a couple that caught their attention. The profile showed a couple named Erin and Jamal, both in their early thirties, a lot younger than Mike and Sam. They seemed to have an easygoing, adventurous vibe and were an interracial couple, just like Andre and his wife.

Their message was warm and inviting, expressing a mutual interest and excitement in meeting.

Mike raised his eyebrows as he read the message aloud. "They're asking if we want to meet up for drinks this weekend." He glanced at Sam, a faint grin playing on his lips. "What do you think?"

"I think... I think we should go for it."

They messaged Erin and Jamal back, arranging a casual meetup at a local bar that coming Friday. When the day arrived, Sam found herself feeling both nervous and excited, choosing an outfit that was just suggestive enough, wanting to feel attractive and confident. Mike gave her an encouraging smile as they left the house, his hand resting reassuringly on her back as they made their way to the bar.

CHAPTER TWENTY-FIVE:
Rekindling the Thrill

Sam adjusted her dress nervously as she and Mike walked into the dimly lit bar. Her heart was pounding, excitement and nerves rushing through her. This would be the first time that since Andre that they would be getting involved with another couple that they had only spoken with online. She could only hope that this would go better than that time.

Erin and Jamal were already there, seated at a cozy booth near the back. Erin greeted them with a warm smile, her blonde curls bouncing as she waved them over, while Jamal extended a hand in greeting, Mike catching it first.

"Hey, you must be Sam and Mike!" Erin greeted them, sliding out of the booth to shake their hands. She was petite and energetic, with a welcoming smile, blonde hair and a natural warmth that made Sam feel instantly comfortable. Her partner, Jamal, stood up next to her, tall and broad-shouldered with an effortless charm about him. He had a fade and a relaxed, charismatic energy that Sam couldn't help but notice right away.

"Nice to finally meet you both," Jamal said, shaking Mike's hand firmly and then Sam's. His smile was easygoing, the kind that instantly put people at ease. "We've been looking forward to this."

They all settled into the booth, Mike and Sam sitting across from Erin and Jamal. A waitress came by, taking their drink orders, Sam opted for a glass of wine, while Mike ordered a beer. She noticed that Erin and Jamal were both sipping cocktails, looking completely at ease as they leaned back and smiled at them.

"So, how are you both feeling?" Erin asked with a grin, breaking the ice. "Nervous? Excited?"

Sam laughed. "A bit of both, to be honest," she admitted. "It's nothing new to us but we've been out of the game for a while if we're being honest."

Jamal chuckled. "You're not alone there. It took us a while to figure out what we were both comfortable with and that caused us to take a lot of breaks but now it's something we both enjoy. There's really no pressure, we're just here to see if there's a connection and have a good time."

Erin nodded, reaching over to give Jamal's hand a gentle squeeze. "It's all about having fun, you know? We want you both to feel at ease. This isn't about expectations or anything, it's just a chance to get to know each other."

Sam appreciated how straightforward they were. It felt refreshing, like she didn't have to hide her curiosity or excitement. She exchanged a glance with Mike, who gave her a reassuring smile before turning to Erin and Jamal.

"So, you guys have done this a few times, I take it?" Mike asked, sounding genuinely curious.

Erin nodded, laughing lightly. "Yeah, we have a bit of experience with it. Honestly, it's been a fun way for us to explore things together while keeping our own boundaries clear."
Sam took a sip of her wine. "What kind of boundaries, if you don't mind me asking?"

"Oh, not at all," Erin replied easily. "For me, I like to watch more than anything. Jamal... well, he's the one who usually gets involved, and I love seeing him enjoy himself." She glanced at Jamal with a playful smile and he chuckled, reaching over to give her hand a squeeze.

Jamal leaned in a bit, his gaze resting on Sam with a subtle spark of interest. "And what about you two? What drew you to this?"

Sam hesitated, glancing at Mike. They'd talked about this, of course, but putting it into words still felt strange. "Well... we've been through a lot this past year," she began, choosing her words carefully. "There were some... situations that opened our eyes to different things we didn't know we might like. And we thought... why not try something new together?"

Mike nodded, chiming in. "Yeah, it was kind of unexpected but we realized it brought us closer in some ways. We're just... exploring, I guess."
Erin smiled, nodding as if she understood completely. "It sounds like you two are on the same page. That's the most important thing."

Sam felt herself relaxing more and more, the initial nerves replaced by a genuine interest in Erin and Jamal's experiences. She found herself drawn to Jamal's easygoing charm, his looks and how authentic he was with Erin. She could see why Erin was so supportive of his role in their dynamic, his confidence was magnetic, almost impossible to resist.

At one point, Jamal leaned in, his gaze lingering on Sam. "So, Sam," he said with a playful grin. "What do you think so far? Not too intimidating, I hope?"

She laughed, feeling a faint blush creep up her cheeks. "Not at all," she replied honestly. "Actually, it's… nice. I feel like we're all just here to enjoy each other's company."

Erin nodded in agreement, her eyes twinkling with amusement. "Exactly. That's the whole point. Just good company, good conversation, and seeing where things go."
Mike chuckled, giving Sam's hand a gentle squeeze under the table. She glanced at him, he seemed at ease too, and she could tell he was enjoying the atmosphere.

"So," Sam ventured, "I noticed that you, Erin, mentioned you like to watch Jamal rather than join in. Is that… just a preference?"

Erin smiled, glancing over at Jamal. "Yeah, it's definitely a preference. But there's more to it than that." She shoved Jamal in the sides, as if encouraging him to explain further.

Jamal cleared his throat, looking directly at Sam and Mike with an easy smile. "You could say it's partly because there are... certain things I enjoy that Erin isn't really into. It's actually why this works so well for us."

Sam tilted her head, curiosity piqued. "What do you mean?"

"Well," Erin began, looking to Jamal to see if he wanted to elaborate. "He has, let's say... certain tastes."
Sam furrowed her brow, glancing between them, unsure what they were getting at. "Tastes? Like... preferences?"

Jamal nodded, a slight grin playing at the corner of his mouth. "Yeah, I guess you could say that. I'm into... light BDSM."

"BDSM?" Sam repeated, blinking as she tried to process what he'd just said. She wasn't sure what she had expected but that word caught her off guard. Her cheeks warmed slightly, and she looked to Mike, who seemed equally intrigued, though not exactly surprised. Turning back to Jamal, she managed, "Oh. I see."

But truthfully, she didn't see. Sam wasn't sure how she felt about it. BDSM wasn't something she'd ever imagined herself exploring. To her, it seemed so extreme. Just the thought of it made her feel slightly uncomfortable, even a bit nervous.

Sensing her hesitation, Jamal gave her an understanding nod. "It's not for everyone, I know," he said. "It's something Erin and I are really open about and it's also why she prefers to watch rather than participate. It's just not her thing, and that's totally fine."

Erin nodded, adding, "Exactly. I love seeing him happy, and this arrangement lets us both enjoy ourselves in our own way."

Sam fidgeted slightly. The thought of engaging with something so outside her comfort zone made her want to retreat. She turned to Mike, meeting his gaze with a look that said, 'I'm not sure about this.'

Sensing her discomfort, Mike placed a reassuring hand on her back. "We don't have to do anything we're not comfortable with, Sam," he said gently. "It's all up to us."

She nodded, her nerves easing slightly but not completely. "Yeah, it's just... new for me. I'm not sure how I feel about it."

Jamal nodded, his expression friendly and understanding. "I get it. We didn't mean to make you uncomfortable. It's something we're open about, but it's totally okay if it's not something you're interested in."

Sam exhaled, feeling a bit relieved but still flustered. "Thank you. I just don't know if I'm ready for that kind of thing."

Erin smiled reassuringly. "No pressure at all. We totally understand."

As they continued their conversation, the mood shifted back to something lighter but Sam still felt a little uncertain. She knew that this was all about exploring new possibilities but BDSM? That idea left her feeling so out of her depth. She and Mike would have to have a long talk about where their boundaries truly lay.

Eventually, Erin glanced at the time and smiled at Sam and Mike. "This was a lot of fun," she said warmly. "I think we should do this again sometime, no pressure, of course. Just whenever you both feel comfortable

Jamal nodded, giving them a friendly smile. "Yeah, this was a great first step. We'd love to get to know you two even more."

"I think we'd like that," she replied, glancing at Mike for confirmation. He nodded in agreement, a small smile playing on his lips.

By the end of the night, they'd all agreed to meet again. Walking back to the car, Sam felt different emotions. She felt excitement, she felt curiosity and the underlying uncertainty about getting involved with Jamal and Erin.

But at least she was exploring this with Mike. She glanced over at him, squeezing his hand when they reached the car. "Thank you," she said softly. "For being willing to try this."

He squeezed her hand back, a faint smile on his lips. "Anything for you, Sam. Let's see where this takes us."

CHAPTER TWENTYSIX: The Orgy

Sam found herself oscillating between curiosity to try out this thing with Jamal and hesitation over how it would go.. Jamal had been patient, sensing her reluctance but never pushing her further than she was ready for. Instead, he tried easing her into the idea in his own gentle way.

One day, her phone pinged with a message from Jamal. When she opened it, there was a video, along with a short, reassuring note: 'Nothing intense, just a taste. Let me know what you think.'

Sam hesitated, glancing around to make sure she was alone before pressing play. The video started with a softly lit scene, nothing too intense or overly dramatic. It showed a man and woman, both fully clothed at first, with the woman's wrists gently tied with silk. The man was attentive and careful and he adjusted the ties, checking that she was comfortable. The atmosphere seemed more about trust than anything else. It felt almost artistic, with nothing harsh or aggressive.

As Sam watched, she noticed the subtle way the woman responded to the restraint, her breathing slowing as if she was giving in to the moment. She noticed how the man kept his focus on her, making sure she was okay every step of the way. There was a sense of connection between them, a balance of control and tenderness. It wasn't the harsh image Sam might've had in mind when she first thought about 'BDSM', instead, there was almost an intimacy she hadn't expected.

The video ended with the woman smiling, her head resting on the man's shoulder, and Sam found herself exhaling, feeling oddly turned on.

When her phone pinged again, it was another message from him: 'There's more to it than people think. It's about trust and connection, not just control. But we only do what you're comfortable with.'
Sam found herself smiling a little. She watched the video again, noticing more details. She still felt hesitant but there was no denying that a part of her was curious, maybe even... intrigued.

Then, she got another text from Jamal, this time inviting her to meet him in a hotel. He promised her a safe and comfortable space, assuring her he wouldn't push any boundaries she wasn't ready for. Sam thought about it, her mind going back to the video. This was definitely different from everything she had experienced so far and the thought of experiencing it with Jamal was certainly tempting.

Sam walked into the hotel, her heart racing. As she walked through the lobby, she tried to remind herseld to breathe, to stay calm. She walked over to the receptionist, inquiring about Jamal's room number.

She was directed to his room after they placed a call to him to confirm that he was waiting for someone. When she stepped into the room, she found Jamal waiting for her.

"Hey there," he said, smiling as he stepped forward to greet her. "I'm so glad you came."

He gently took her shoes off, kneeling down in front of her and looking up with those kind eyes. She felt a flutter in her stomach as he moved with care, as if he was treating her like something precious.

"Let's get you comfortable," he said, guiding her to the bed while soft music played in the background.

Sam sat on the edge of the bed. Jamal took her hands, looking into her eyes. "How about a massage? Just to help you relax?"

She nodded, grateful for his thoughtfulness. As he worked on her shoulders, his hands were firm and gentle, kneading away all the tension in her muscles. She let out a soft sigh, feeling herself begin to unwind under his touch.

After a few moments of silence, Sam hesitated, then spoke up. "I just want to say, I'm still worried about the whole BDSM thing. It's so new to me."

Jamal paused, his hands still resting on her back. "I completely understand," he replied softly. "We don't have to dive into that tonight if you're not ready. We can take it slow."

"Really?" she asked, looking back at him.

"Absolutely," he said, a reassuring smile on his face. "You're beautiful just the way you are. I wouldn't need anything else to get off. It's all about making you feel comfortable."

His words sent a wave of warmth through her and she felt a little more at ease. "Thank you. I just..."

"Shh," he interrupted gently, leaning down to place a kiss on her shoulder. "Let's just enjoy this moment."

He continued the massage, his hands moving down her back, loosening her muscles further. Sam closed her eyes, focusing on the sensations, no doubt about it, she felt safe. A complete 180 from how she felt with Tyrell.

After a while, Jamal's hands moved to her waist, slowly sliding around to her front. He leaned in closer, his breath warm against her skin. "How does this feel?"

"Really good," she admitted, feeling her breath hitch a little.

"Good," he murmured, his hands gliding up to her breasts, gently cupping them. The sensation sent shivers through her body. "Just relax. Let me take care of you."

Sam let out a breathy sigh, feeling herself melting into the bed. Jamal was soft handed but there was this subtle possession in it. He leaned over and took her lips into a soft kiss, not the harsh ones she would usually get from the other men she had booked Jo with but a genuine, slow, sweet kiss. And she kissed him back, eagerly.

As their kisses grew more heated, Jamal pulled back slightly, his eyes dark. "I want to try something, okay? Just to ease you into the idea of kink."

Her heart raced at the thought but she felt curious, too. "What do you mean?"

He smiled, reaching for a soft scarf that lay on the bedside table. "I'd like to tie your arms back a little. Just to see how it feels. I promise it won't be anything crazy."

Sam's breath caught in her throat, her hesitation creeping back. But looking into his eyes, she could see the sincerity there. "Okay," she said, though her voice trembled slightly.

Jamal took the scarf and gently wrapped it around her wrists, securing them to the headboard of the bed. "How's that?" he asked, checking in on her.

"Not too tight," she replied, surprised at how secure it felt without being uncomfortable.

"Perfect," he said, his smile returning. He leaned in again, kissing her softly before trailing his lips down her neck. Sam shivered at his touch, the anticipation swirling in her stomach.

Then, Jamal reached for a small vibrator that had been lying on the bedside table. "I want to add this into the mix. Just to heighten the pleasure a bit."

"What do I do?" Sam asked, excitement and nervousness bubbling inside her.

"Just let go," he said, turning it on and placing it against her sensitive skin. The vibrations sent wave after wave of pleasurable sensations through her body, causing her to gasp.

When did she become so sensitive?

"Oh..." Sam gasped, her body arching towards him, instinctively craving more.

"Just like that," he encouraged, watching her reaction. "Let me know what feels good."

He continued to kiss her, moving lower, his lips tracing a path down her body. The combination of the vibrations and his mouth on her skin sent her mind spinning. She felt exhilarated and also strangely vulnerable, a strange mix that terrified and thrilled her.

"Jamal..." she breathed, her voice shaky but he only smiled against her skin, focusing on her pleasure.

Just when it felt like she was about to let go, Jamal began giving her light spanks on the side of her body as she changed the speed from the vibrator. He was testing her limits while still keeping it light.

"Does that feel good?" he asked.

"Yes," she gasped, her body responding to every touch, every kiss, every playful smack.

Jamal continued to play with her boundaries, making it clear that he has no plans of penetrating her. His whole plan here was to get her to calm down and see that there was nothing scary about BDSM.

And it looked like his plan was working.

Just as quickly as he started this session, he ended it. Sam looked at him with glazed eyes, wondering why he stopped.

He smiled shyly and said, "If I went any further, I might have to do something I wasn't planning on doing tonight."

He gave a pointed look downward and Sam's eyes opened in shock when she saw the massive tent pitched in his pants. Had she done that to him? Driven him to this point of excruciating pleasure. She could see it throbbing already.

"I hope you'll give me another chance to do this. I would really like to fuck you next time." He whispered, leaning down and giving her a slight kiss.

Jamal had shown Sam a different side of intimacy and she couldn't shake the smile off her face as she left the hotel, her heart still racing from the experience.

Later that evening, she found herself sitting on the couch with Mike, who was catching up on some sports highlights. He glanced over at her, noticing the way she was practically glowing. "You seem happy. Did you have a good time today?" he asked.

"I did," Sam admitted, her cheeks warming at the thought of Jamal. "Really good, actually."

Mike raised an eyebrow, intrigued. "Good to hear. Are you feeling ready to... explore more with him?"

Just then, her phone buzzed, interrupting their conversation. It was a message from Jamal: "Hey, how about you and Mike come over tonight? We can chill and discuss our new dynamic. It'll be fun!"

Sam felt a rush of excitement at the idea. "Jamal wants us to come over tonight," she said, biting her lip.

"Sounds like a good idea," Mike replied. "You enjoyed your time with him, right?"

"Definitely," she said, nodding vigorously. "He really helped me feel more comfortable."

"Then let's go," Mike said with a nod. "I trust you, and it'll be nice to see how we can make this work together."

The atmosphere in Jamal's apartment was calm. When they knocked, Jamal welcomed them with open arms, his charm radiating as he greeted them both.

"Glad you could make it!" he said, his smile infectious. "I thought we could start with some drinks and just hang out for a bit."

They settled into the cozy living room, drinks in hand, as the conversation flowed easily. Jamal was watching Sam intently as she sipped on her drink and she didn't know whether to feel uncomfortable or flattered.

After a while, Jamal leaned back, a thoughtful expression on his face. "You know, I really enjoyed our last session, Sam. You have such incredible body."

"Thanks," she said, her cheeks warming at the compliment. "I really appreciate how patient you've been with me."

He smiled, leaning in closer. "It's easy when you're so receptive. And I think there's more we can explore together."

Mike, sitting beside Sam, watched the exchange. "What do you have in mind?" he asked, leaning forward slightly, clearly interested in where this was heading.

Jamal's gaze flicked between them, "Well, we can start with something simple. Just some light teasing, a little playfulness. I think Sam would enjoy it."

"What do you mean?" Sam asked.

Jamal smiled, his voice low and inviting. "Let's have some fun. How about a little game? I want to see how well I can push your limits, Sam. With Mike's permission, of course."

Mike nodded, clearly intrigued. "I'm open to seeing where this goes."

With that encouragement, Jamal stood up, extending his hand to Sam. "Come on, let's move to the bedroom. It'll be more comfortable there."

Sam took his hand, her pulse quickening as she followed him into the bedroom. He led her to the bed then made her sit in it, after which he turned to face her.

"Let's start with something simple," he said. "Just lie back and relax. I want to see how you respond to a little teasing."

He leaned down, brushing his lips softly against her skin, and Sam felt a thrill run through her.

"You're so sensitive Sam, I love it. Just focus on the sensations," he instructed. "Let everything else fade away."

He began to kiss her neck, moving down her collarbone. She closed her eyes, surrendering to the moment as Jamal explored her body, his kisses trailing lower.

"Sam, you can tell me to stop at any time," he murmured, flicking his tongue down the indent in her collarbone. "But I want to see how far we can take this."

Just then, Mike walked in, watching the scene unfold. Sam glanced over at him, her heart racing as she realized he was fully aware of what was happening.

Jamal paused for a moment, locking eyes with Mike. "Is this okay with you?" he asked, ensuring they were both on the same page.

Mike nodded, his expression filled with a hint of desire. "Yeah, I'm good with it," he replied, leaning against the doorframe.

Encouraged by Mike's approval, Jamal turned his attention back to Sam, a wicked grin on his face. "Let's kick it up a notch, shall we?"

With that, he grabbed the scarf he had used before, gently binding her wrists again. Sam felt a thrill at the idea of being restrained, her heart racing as Jamal took control.
"Just relax and enjoy," he said, teasing her lips with his. "I promise you'll love this."

Mike watched intently as Jamal tied his wife's wrist to the headboard then knelt in between her thighs, opening them up for him. Slowly, Jamal's hand went up and down Sam's thigh, squeezing, pinching, sending different sensations through her, causing her to make a variety of sounds.

Jamal chuckled to himself, "This would be so much better if you were blindfolded." He turned to Mike then pointed to the dresser next to the bed, "Could you get the blindfold out of there, please? Don't just stand there and watch."

Mike blinked, like he was surprised he was suddenly a part of this now but he walked over to the dresser and took out the blindfold. He handed it to Jamal but he shook his head.

"Put it on her, put the blindfold on your wife Mike." Jamal said, his voice dangerously low.

Mike obeyed and knelt on the bed by Sam's head, slipping the blindfold on her. He turned to Jamal, who was smiling by this point.

"Now you get to watch me take your wife." he whispered, settling himself between Sam's thighs then burying his face in them. Sam buckled instantly, feeling his warm, wet tongue stroke the tip of her clit. Jamal wasn't aggressive about it or anything, he was slow and gentle like he was savoring the taste of her.

Sam tugged at the restraints her wrists were in, wanting to grab onto Jamal's head because of how overwhelming the sensations he was giving her was. Jamal's tongue circled and flicked against the head of her clit, making a sucking motion at the same time.

While he did that, he brought his finger over and slipped one then two into her. He moved his finger within her, earning moans from her. Sam began to buck her hips against his fingers, trying her hardest to cum against them.

Jamal came up for air, his mouth glistening from Sam's juices. "You should join us Mike, I think Sam would like to give you a blowjob. Isn't that right Sam?"

Mike looked over at Sam, wondering if that was what she really wanted but she looked so flushed and breathless that he wasn't sure she would even be able to speak.

Still though, he unbuckled his pants and revealed his boner, one that had come on from watching Jamal eat his wife out. He pressed his dick into her mouth and she opened up for him, causing him to moan as the head of his dick got enveloped by her mouth.

Sam moaned and tried to bob her head as best as she could, up and down the shaft. Jamal watched them go at it for a while before burying his face back into Sam's thighs, lapping at her clit once again.

Erin came in at that moment and stood by the doorframe, watching them intently. Mike was shoving his penis down Sam's throat while her husband licked her up and tried to make her cum with his fingers.

The sight turned her on.

Careful not to alert them to her presence, she walked over to the closet across the bed and took out a purple vibrator before walking over to a nearby chair where she could watch all three of them go at it.

She took off her shorts, spread her legs then brought the vibrator to her clit, turning it on. The vibration instantly caused her to throw her head back as shock waves went through her body.

The sound of the vibrator drew Mike's attention and he watched as Erin threw her head back, covering her mouth with one hand whilst the other held the vibrator she used to pleasure herself. If he was hard before then he was even harder now, unable to take his eyes off her as she moved her hips against the vibrator.

Sam, at that moment, was reaching the edge. She was so overcome by what Jamal was doing to her that she had no choice but to let go. Jamal used his thumb to circle her clit which caused her to finally lose control, and she let out a strained moan even as Mike's dick was in her mouth.

Jamal got back on his knees and looked at Sam, whose head was rolled back, no longer pleasuring Mike. He turned to the direction of where the vibration was coming from and saw his wife right in the thick of getting herself off. At that moment he got a sneaky idea.

He undid Sam's restraints, turning her on her stomach with the intention of taking her from behind. Meanwhile he felt his wife could not miss out on the fun so he asked Mike to join her so the both of them could watch him and Sam go at it.

Sam was out of breath but not enough to miss out on the chance to fuck Jamal. He gave her a light smack on her asss then propped her up on her knees so she was arching in front of him, her ass and pussy in full view.

"Gosh, I want to bury my face in there again." He said, as he brought his dick up to her entrance for the first time. "But I'm going to savor this even more."

Jamal groaned as he slid into Sam slowly. She winced as she was extra sensitive down there but she started to moan when he moved within her, savoring the way her walls drew him in.

"Fuckkk," he whispered as he thrusted into Sam repeatedly. He gripped onto her hips as hard as he could and watched as each slap from his body caused hers to jiggle. He wanted to go deeper, harder, faster but he knew he had to pace himself.

By this time, Mike was besides Erin, stroking himself whilst she got herself off with the vibrator. She put the vibrator down then looked at Mike as he stroked himself while he watched Jamal fuck his wife.

"You know what's even better than a vibrator?" she said all of a sudden, drawing Mike's attention away from the other two.

"What?" Mike asked.

"Real dick." she said, as she tipped her finger to summon him over to her. Under normal circumstances, Mike would hesitate but he couldn't at this point not when he was so horny.

Without wasting any time, he was in front of Erin and within her in a moment, slapping into her hard and reckless, nothing like the refined strokes from Jamal. Erin didn't seem to care though, she held onto Mike and moaned out loud as he drove himself into her.

The smacking from their bodies drew Jamal's attention and he smirked when he realized that his plan had worked after all. Jamal made his thrusts more intense, not to be outmatched by the erratic thrusts from Mike.

He leaned over and pounded into Sam repeatedly, she was so wet and so
warm, the sound of all the bodies slapping into each other was driving him crazy. Just as he felt like he was about to lose control, he heard groans coming from the corner and out of the corner of his eye, he saw Mike and Erin cumming together.

That was enough to get him where he wanted to go and he groaned deeply as he gave two more really intense thrusts before pulling out and cumming all over the sheets.

He tried to catch his breath as the spasms faded away then smacked Sam's ass again just for the fun of it before collapsing on the bed, out of breath.

"I gotta say, you white people know how to wear a guy out." he said, chuckling.

All four of them crawled into bed and before either knew what was happening, they were fast asleep, exhausted from the sex and the orgasms.

THE END

Dear reader,

Thank you for reading to the end! I hope the book lived up to your expectations!

Exclusive erotic short story club
Want even more? You can join my exclusive erotic short club **for free**. By doing so, you will get a bunch of free stories (before I publish them), audiobook coupon codes, and much more! Join here: https://bit.ly/3WJsqRp

Or email me at amber.carden.books@gmail.com and I will send you a link!

Amber

© **Copyright 2024 - All rights reserved.**

The content contained within this book may not be reproduced, duplicated, or transmitted without direct written permission from the author or the publisher.

This book is copyright protected. It is only for personal use. You cannot amend, distribute, sell, use, quote or paraphrase any part, or the content within this book, without the consent of the author or publisher.

www.ingramcontent.com/pod-product-compliance
Lightning Source LLC
LaVergne TN
LVHW041942070526
838199LV00051BA/2883